TANGLED HEARTS

TANGLED BOOK TWO

AASKA SHAH

To the ones who have loved deeply, lost painfully, and still dared to believe in love again.

Contents

Contents

Contents

Contents

Foreword

Love is rarely simple. It twists, it turns, it tangles—yet somehow, it always finds its way back to where it belongs. Tangled Hearts is a story of love in its most raw and unfiltered form, where emotions run deep, choices shape destinies, and hearts learn to navigate the delicate balance between longing and letting go.

Writing this book has been a journey of its own, one that has allowed me to explore the complexities of love, relationships, and the unspoken emotions that reside within us all. Through Aarna, Ayaan and Rishi's story, I hope to capture the essence of those fleeting yet profound moments that define our connections with others.

This book is for anyone who has ever felt the rush of first love, the sting of heartbreak, and the hope of a second chance. To my readers, thank you for embarking on this journey with me. May you find pieces of your own heart within these pages.

With love and gratitude,

[Aaska]

Preface

Every love story has its own rhythm—some are slow and steady, while others burn brightly before fading into memory. Some are woven with laughter and joy, while others are marked by pain and longing. But no matter the course they take, all love stories leave behind a trace, a lingering emotion that shapes the people who experience them. Tangled Hearts is one such story—a journey of love that defies time, a story of emotions that persist despite distance, and of two souls constantly finding and losing each other, only to realize that love, in its truest form, is never truly lost.

This book was born from the desire to explore the nuances of love—not just the grand gestures or the dramatic reunions, but the quiet moments, the hesitations, the miscommunications, and the deep yearning that often goes unspoken. Love is rarely perfect; it is raw, messy, and sometimes heartbreakingly complicated. Yet, it is also one of the most profound and transformative experiences a person can have. Through the journey of Aarna and Rishi, I wanted to capture the fragility and resilience of the human heart, the beauty of connection, and the pain of separation. Their story is a reflection of the countless relationships that ebb and flow, reminding us that sometimes, love is about timing, about choices, and about learning to embrace both the joy and the sorrow it brings.

As you turn these pages, I hope you feel the heartbeats of the characters, their struggles, their triumphs, and their silent battles. I hope you resonate with their longing, their dreams, and the bittersweet nature of love itself. Love is never a straight path—it twists and turns, leading us to places we never expected. And yet, it is in these twists and turns that we discover the depths of our own hearts and the truths that shape our destinies.

Thank you for choosing to embark on this journey with me. May Tangled Hearts stay with you long after the last page is turned, reminding you that no matter how tangled love may seem, it always finds its way.

Acknowledgements

Writing Tangled Hearts has been a journey filled with emotions, reflections, and endless moments of self-discovery. This book would not have been possible without the love and support of so many incredible people, to whom I owe my deepest gratitude.

First and foremost, to my family—your unwavering belief in me has been my greatest strength. Thank you for your patience, encouragement, and for always pushing me to follow my dreams. Your love is the foundation on which this book stands.

To my friends, who have been my constant cheerleaders, thank you for listening to my ideas, for reading my drafts, and for reminding me why I started this journey in the first place. Your words of motivation and your presence in my life mean more than I can ever express.

To my readers—whether this is the first book of mine you're reading or you've been on this journey with me before—thank you. Your love for stories, your messages, and your unwavering support inspire me to keep writing. This book is for you.

Lastly, to love itself—the inspiration behind Tangled Hearts. For all its beauty, complexity, and unpredictability, love is what makes life worth living. And for that, I am forever grateful.

Prologue

Love is a paradox—gentle yet fierce, simple yet complicated. It has the power to heal and the power to break, often at the same time.

Aarna had always believed that love was meant to be soft, like the pages of an old book, delicate yet full of stories waiting to be told. But life had a way of proving her wrong. She had known love, felt it slip through her fingers, and watched it return like waves to the shore—sometimes calm, sometimes turbulent.

Rishi had never been afraid of love, yet he had spent years trying to understand it. He believed that love wasn't about perfection, but about persistence. And Aarna—she had been both his greatest joy and his deepest ache.

Ayaan, on the other hand, was the enigma that neither Aarna nor Rishi could fully decipher. He had been the steady presence, the unwavering support, and yet, somewhere along the way, he had changed. His love was different—silent, restrained, filled with unspoken words and hidden pain. His presence had always lingered in the background of their story, shaping their choices in ways they never quite understood.

Their love was never meant to be simple. It was tangled in memories, in moments of longing and hesitation, in the things they said and the things they left unsaid. But in the end, love was never about being easy—it was about being real.

This is their story. A story of hearts that strayed yet remained tethered, of love that fought against time and distance, of a connection too strong to be severed.

Because sometimes, no matter how tangled love gets, it always finds its way back.

xvi

1

AARNA

March 20, 2022

Dear Diary,

Today has been one of those calm, beautiful days that make you feel like the universe is on your side. The weather was perfect—a gentle breeze, a clear blue sky, and the kind of sunlight that feels like a warm hug. I spent most of the morning reorganizing my desk and putting up a few Polaroids of my favorite moments from the past year. Later, I took a long walk around the campus, letting myself soak in the beauty of this place I now call home.

It's funny how life has a way of surprising you when you least expect it. If someone had told me a year ago that I'd be here—standing at the edge of my dreams, finally stepping into the future I've always envisioned—I would have laughed. But here I am, writing this entry from my cozy little desk at St. Clair's College, my dream college. I'm still pinching myself to believe it's real.

These last few months have been a whirlwind. It all started with the board results. I still remember the knot in my stomach as I logged in to check my score. Third in school! I could almost hear Mom's proud laughter echo in the room. That moment was mine, something I'd earned with sleepless nights, endless revisions, and my unwavering determination. It was a validation—proof that focusing on myself was worth it.

College life has been a revelation. St. Clair's is everything I'd dreamed of and more. The sprawling campus, the late-night study sessions, the endless cups of coffee—it feels like a movie. For the first time in years, I'm truly investing in myself.

Skincare, fitness, career—three words that have become my mantra. I've started a proper skincare routine now (thanks to Simie's endless tips), and I've even joined the college's yoga club. Every morning, I feel lighter, stronger, and… dare I say it, happier. And my career? I'm finally able to focus on commerce without distractions. It feels like I'm building the foundation for something big—something mine.

Speaking of Simie, she's one of the best parts of this new chapter. Our friendship has only grown deeper. She's still the bubbly, optimistic girl who never lets me take life too seriously. And then there's Vihaan and who would've thought that this boy who I started talking as random group project partners would become such an integral part of my life?

Sometimes, though, on quiet evenings like this, I find myself thinking about Rishi. It's not as painful as it used to be, but there are moments—when I hear a Taylor Swift song or watch a heartwarming Bollywood movie—when I can't help but wonder what it would be like if he were still part of my life. Would he tease me about my yoga poses or complain about my taste in movies? I don't dwell on it for long, though. I've accepted that some things aren't meant to be, and that's okay. Life moves on, and so have I. What we had was beautiful, but it's part of my past now, not my future.

But most importantly, I've learned to enjoy my own company. I've started journaling regularly—not just to vent, but to understand myself better. Writing down my thoughts has become a therapy of sorts, helping me untangle the knots in my mind and make sense of my emotions. It's like having a heart-to-heart conversation with myself. And you know what, Diary? I'm not so bad to talk to after all.

As I write this, the golden rays of the evening sun are streaming through the window, casting a warm glow on my little world. It's moments like these that make me realize how far I've come. I'm finally living for myself—not for anyone else, not for expectations, not for the past. Just for me.

Here's to new beginnings, new dreams, and a future that's as bright as this sunset.

Love,
Aarna

2

AARNA

The soft pitter-patter of rain on the windowpane woke me up this morning. There's something magical about the monsoons—the way the earth smells after the first rain, the lush greenery that seems to come alive, and the symphony of raindrops falling in perfect harmony. It's like nature's way of reminding us to pause and appreciate its beauty.

I stretched lazily, letting the cool breeze coming in through the slightly open window wash over me. Today felt special, though I couldn't quite put my finger on why. As I got ready for college, I picked out my favorite yellow chikankari kurta. It always felt like sunshine on a rainy day, and I paired it with my silver jhumkas—a small touch of elegance that always made me feel confident.

"Your coffee, Aaru," Mom's voice called out from the kitchen. She always made the perfect cup of coffee—just the right amount of sugar and a sprinkle of love. I took a sip, savoring the warmth that spread through me. "Thanks, Mom. You're the best," I said, giving her a quick hug before heading out.

The rains had turned the city into a maze of puddles. As I stepped out, the air was cool and refreshing, carrying the scent of wet earth. I hailed an auto and hopped in, holding my bag close to keep it dry. The roads were crowded with people clutching umbrellas, dodging puddles, and rushing to their destinations. It was chaos, but there was a certain charm to it—the kind that only monsoon mornings could bring.

When we reached the college gate, I rummaged through my bag to find change for the fare. As I stepped down, distracted by my search, I accidentally bumped into someone.

"Watch where you're going," the man said curtly, brushing past me without so much as a second glance. He was tall, dressed in a blazer, and radiated an air of self-importance. His sharp brown eyes barely acknowledged me as he strode away, leaving me stunned and, frankly, annoyed.

Before I could say anything, my foot slipped on the wet pavement, and I landed squarely in a puddle. I looked up, half expecting him to turn back and help, but he didn't. Instead, he disappeared into the crowd, indifferent to the mess he'd left behind.

Embarrassment and frustration flooded my cheeks as I struggled to get up, my hands and kurta now soaked and muddy. My favorite yellow chikankari kurta was ruined, and I felt a lump rise in my throat. The auto driver, noticing my predicament, handed me a rag to wipe my hands.

"Thank you," I mumbled, handing him the fare before heading toward the college gates. My heart sank a little as I walked, feeling self-conscious about my disheveled state. The rain, which had felt magical just an hour ago, now seemed more like a nuisance.

As I made my way to class, I couldn't help but glance down at the wet stains on my kurta and sigh. Maybe today wasn't so special after all.

3

AYAAN

I've never been the type to get distracted. College wasn't the place for that. I'd worked too damn hard to get here, poured hours into books and practice exams, just to make sure my future was secure. Women? They were distractions—nothing more. And I wasn't about to let some pretty face mess with everything I'd worked for.

But then, I saw her.

I don't even know what caught my attention at first. Maybe it was the yellow of her chikankari kurta, bright and cheerful against the sea of drab colors everyone else was wearing. Maybe it was the way the intricate patterns of the fabric seemed to shimmer in the sunlight, catching the light just right. Or maybe it was the sound—the soft tinkling of silver jhumkhas swaying with every step she took. They made this tiny musical chime that somehow cut through the usual noise of campus.

Whatever it was, I couldn't look away. I told myself I should, but it was like my eyes were glued to her. She was standing there, caught in her own world, walking with a kind of grace that almost felt... too perfect.

I shook my head, trying to focus. I had a lecture to attend, notes to review, and a whole life to build. I didn't need distractions. So I started walking, trying to ignore the pull of curiosity. But then—slosh—I heard the sound of feet slipping, and before I could even process it, she was falling.

One moment, she was walking, looking like she belonged in a painting, and the next, she was sprawled on the ground, her knees slamming into the puddle with a harsh thud.

I froze.

Her jhumkhas—the ones I'd noticed earlier—spun through the air, landing somewhere in the water with a soft, hollow sound. And there she was, sitting in the puddle, staring at the mess she'd made, her face flushed with embarrassment.

I didn't move. I don't even know why. Part of me wanted to go over, make sure she was okay, but another part of me knew that wasn't my problem. I wasn't the guy who jumped in to save anyone. I wasn't that guy.

But damn, there was something about the way she looked. The soft curve of her face, the way she tried to get up, the innocence in those wide brown eyes—it was like she was caught in a moment of vulnerability, and I just couldn't look away.

I shook my head, trying to snap myself out of it. This wasn't my problem. I wasn't here to play the hero. So, I kept walking, past her, pretending I didn't notice the way her hand brushed against the puddle, the way her hair fell over her face as she tried to stand up.

But even as I entered the lecture hall, I couldn't shake the image of her from my mind. The yellow kurta, the jhumkhas, the big brown eyes. I sat down at my desk, pulling out my notes, trying to focus on the lecture, but I couldn't do it. My mind kept drifting back to her. Focus, Ayaan, I told myself. You have a future to build, a career to secure. One fall, one girl—it doesn't matter.

Professor Tawde's voice sliced through my thoughts. "Alright, everyone. Settle down. Let's start."

I tried to pay attention, but it was useless. I was stuck in a loop of images—her face, her jhumkhas, those eyes that looked so startled when she'd fallen.

And then I heard it.

"Aarna!" Tawde barked, his tone sharp. "For God's sake, how many times do I have to tell you? Your clothes are a disaster. Stains all over the place. This isn't a street market, it's a college. Keep yourself together."

I stopped.

Aarna.

That was her name.

The girl. The one who'd fallen. The one with the jhumkhas and the yellow kurta. Something clicked in my brain, and I felt that familiar, gnawing feeling in my gut.

Aarna was the one getting scolded by Tawde. The one who had stains all over her clothes—stains that, from what I could tell, weren't there when I first saw her. But hearing her name? The realization hit me hard. I'd seen her just moments before, sprawled in that puddle, drenched.

A wave of frustration hit me, but I pushed it aside. Why did I care? Why was I even thinking about her? She was just another student here, probably one of those messy, disorganized types. The kind who always seemed to get in trouble. Not my problem. Not my concern.

But damn, that name kept bouncing around in my head. Aarna.

And those brown eyes—those huge, innocent eyes that made her look like she belonged somewhere far away from here. Somewhere calm. Somewhere safe.

I didn't know why it bothered me so much. I had enough on my plate. I had things to do. Focus on the lecture, Ayaan, I reminded myself. You're here for a reason. You've come too far to get sidetracked by... her.

But even as I scribbled down notes, the sound of jhumkhas and the image of Aarna falling into that puddle wouldn't leave me. And deep down, I hated that it wouldn't.

4

AARNA

The moment I stepped into the classroom, my eyes instinctively drifted to the same guy I had seen in the morning. He sat near the window, his sharp features highlighted by the soft sunlight filtering through the glass. There was something effortlessly attractive about him—the way he leaned back in his chair, his fingers tapping rhythmically on the desk as if lost in thought. I still didn't know his name, and a part of me was too hesitant to ask.

I tore my gaze away, reminding myself that I had other things to worry about. Like the fact that Professor Tawde had just humiliated me in front of the entire class.

Muttering a small apology, I had ducked my head and hurried to the nearest empty seat, wishing I could disappear altogether.

Now, as I settled in the corner of the classroom, I let out a slow breath, trying to shake off the embarrassment still clinging to my skin. My hands reached for my accounting books, and I busied myself flipping through the pages, pretending to be deeply engrossed in the text.

But I couldn't help it. My gaze flickered up, just once, in the direction of the boy by the window. And to my utter dismay, he was already looking at me.

Before I could dwell on it further, Professor Tawde clapped his hands together, silencing the murmurs in the room. "Alright, class. For today's activity, I will be dividing you into groups of five. Work together and ensure everyone contributes. The assignment is a presentation on Partnership Accounts, so you will need to divide the topics amongst yourselves and coordinate efficiently."

As he started calling out names, my heart pounded in anticipation. When he finally reached my group, I heard my name, followed by a few others. And then, the last name—Ayaan.

I glanced up, and sure enough, the guy from the window seat was looking straight at me. So, his name was Ayaan. The realization sent a strange flutter through my chest.

Keeping my face neutral, I nodded slightly as our group gathered together. This was going to be interesting.

We quickly settled around a table, exchanging brief introductions. "I'm Aarna," I said, forcing a polite smile as my eyes briefly met Ayaan's. He gave a small nod. "Ayaan."

The others introduced themselves, and soon, we were discussing the assignment. We decided to split the topics—Ayaan and I were assigned the segment on the dissolution of a partnership, a complicated yet crucial part of the subject.

As the discussion went on, I noticed how Ayaan spoke—calm, confident, and precise. He seemed to know a lot about the topic, which both impressed and intimidated me. I, on the other hand, felt a little flustered, still recovering from my earlier embarrassment.

As the class went on, I couldn't shake off the feeling that this partnership—at least academically—was going to be an experience I wouldn't forget anytime soon.

13

5

AYAAN

I never believed in destiny playing games, but looking at how things were unfolding, I couldn't help but wonder if fate had a twisted sense of humor. Of all the people in class, Aarna had to be in my group. Not that I minded—she was intriguing in an unexpected way—but I couldn't shake off the feeling that this partnership was going to test my patience.

The moment we started discussing the assignment, I realized I had already studied most of the material. Partnership Accounts weren't particularly challenging for me; I had read through dissolution clauses and revaluation concepts long before this discussion even began. But Aarna? She seemed... distracted.

While I was listing out key points and structuring our part of the presentation, she was busy chatting with Kaira at the next table about some web series. Something about a guy named Rishi and how some dimple character threw coffee on him. The sheer absurdity of the topic grated on my nerves. I clenched my jaw, exhaling through my nose, willing myself to ignore the incessant giggles coming from her side.

"Aarna," I finally said, trying to rein in my irritation. "We need to finalize how we're splitting the subtopics."

She blinked, turning back to me as if she had only just remembered I was there. "Oh, right. Yeah. What were we discussing again?"

I ran a hand through my hair, resisting the urge to roll my eyes. This was going to be harder than I thought.

But then, just as I was about to call it a lost cause, I heard it—the soft twinkling of her jhumkas as she tilted her head, waiting for me to speak. It was such a delicate sound, almost like wind chimes in the evening breeze, and oddly enough, it fixed everything.

My irritation faded as quickly as it had come. Shaking my head slightly, I exhaled, deciding to let it go. "Let's just divide it like this..." I said, and surprisingly, she nodded and started taking notes.

Maybe fate really was playing a game. I just wasn't sure if I was ready to find out the rules yet.

AARNA

The assignment had finally come to an end, and to my surprise, Professor Tawde actually appreciated our group's effort. "Well done," he said, adjusting his glasses as he glanced at our final presentation slides. "You all worked well together. An A for your group."

I let out a small breath of relief. Despite the distractions, we had pulled through. As soon as the class ended, Kaira nudged me, her expression more serious than usual.

Kaira was the first friend I had made when I started my CA classes. From the very first day, we just clicked. She was warm, understanding, and had this effortless way of making me feel at home even in a room full of strangers. Over time, she became more than just a friend—she was like a sister to me.

"Aarna, listen," she started, lowering her voice as we stepped out of the classroom. "You need to be careful around Ayaan."

I frowned. "What? Why?"

She sighed, glancing around before continuing. "He's... not the right guy for you. He's got a messy past, Aarna. A reputation for breaking hearts. He's too selfish when it comes to relationships."

I pursed my lips, digesting her words. I wasn't entirely sure what to make of them, but Kaira wasn't the type to spread baseless rumors. If she was warning me, there had to be a reason.

"Alright," I said after a moment. "I'll stay away."

And with that, I pushed the thought of Ayaan aside.

When I reached home that evening, exhausted from the day, I tossed my bag on the bed and collapsed onto the mattress. Just as I was about to close my eyes, my phone buzzed.

A message.

From Rishi.

Hi.

My breath hitched. My hands felt clammy as a familiar wave of panic surged through me. I hadn't spoken to Rishi in a while, and suddenly, a simple text felt like a bomb ticking away in my hands. Without thinking, I grabbed my phone and dialed Simie's number.

She picked up almost instantly. "What happened?"

I took a shaky breath. "Rishi texted me. Just 'hi.' And I don't know what to do."

There was a pause. Then, in her usual calm tone, Simie said, "Aarna, you need to talk to him. You can't keep avoiding this forever."

▷▷▷

7

AYAAN

I wasn't one to believe in fate, but something about the way Aarna kept crossing my path made me question if the universe was playing some elaborate joke on me. The assignment was over, Professor Tawde had given us an A, and I should've been able to move past this phase like any other. But for some reason, I couldn't.

Throughout the presentation, I had expected Aarna to struggle. Not because she lacked intelligence, but because she seemed... detached. Like she was always elsewhere in her head. And yet, when she spoke, there was an odd kind of confidence in her voice. It wasn't rehearsed; it was natural. She explained her points in such an effortless manner that it actually made me listen, despite already knowing most of what she was saying.

And that annoyed me more than it should have.

I wasn't used to being thrown off. I had worked hard to be the best at what I did, to have control over everything I engaged in. But Aarna was unpredictable. One moment she was absentmindedly playing with her pen, the next she was delivering a solid argument about the intricacies of partnership deeds. It was frustrating. It was... intriguing.

After class, I caught her talking to Kaira, her voice a little hushed but still carrying that unmistakable softness. Kaira, on the other hand, looked dead serious. I wasn't the kind of guy to eavesdrop, but the way they glanced in my direction made it clear enough that I was the subject of their conversation.

Aarna's brows furrowed for a brief second before she gave a small nod. A decision made. Then she walked away.

I shook my head. I had no idea what Kaira told her, but I had a feeling I could guess.

Aarna didn't know the full story. Most people didn't. They never cared to ask. And why would they? I had built this mask of arrogance and confidence over the years—an image that protected me from questions, from curiosity. It wasn't like I was proud of my past, but I didn't want to drag anyone into it either. I had made mistakes—things I couldn't undo. Things that made people whisper behind my back, things that created a reputation I couldn't shake.

When I was younger, I was the golden boy—smart, athletic, charming. Everything came easy. That was until I met Tanvi. She was the kind of girl everyone admired—beautiful, intelligent, and popular. I was drawn to her, not because of any deep connection, but because she represented everything I thought I wanted. At first, it was just casual. We'd hang out in the same circle, talk here and there. Then came the parties, the nights that bled into mornings, the little secrets, and the careless decisions. It didn't take long for things to spiral. There were lies, betrayal, and a breaking point where I lost her, lost myself in the process.

When it ended, I was left with a reputation—one of a heartbreaker, a guy who couldn't keep his head on straight. What people didn't know was that I wasn't the only one at fault. Tanvi had her part to play, too, but she was the kind of person who always got a free pass, no questions asked. I wasn't the first guy she'd toyed with, but I was the one who took the fall for it.

And so, the whispers began. My friends, who once had my back, backed away. People I didn't even know started judging me for things they didn't understand. They painted me with broad strokes, and I let them.

The worst part? I didn't even try to explain myself. The truth felt too heavy, too complicated to put into words. So, I buried it, behind the walls of sarcasm and indifference.

Still, I wasn't one to explain myself. If Aarna wanted to stay away, that was fine.

Or at least, that's what I told myself.

Later that evening, as I sat in my room scrolling mindlessly through my phone, I found myself checking our class group chat. Aarna had sent a message about some notes, addressing the entire group, but for some reason, my eyes lingered on her name longer than necessary.

Something about her felt different. She wasn't like the others who'd judged me before. In fact, she seemed almost... unbothered by the rumors. She had that cool, collected demeanor—like she saw through all the noise. She had this quiet confidence, a calmness that set her apart from everyone else. And for some reason, it made me uneasy.

Shaking my head, I tossed my phone aside.

This was ridiculous. I had more important things to focus on.

Yet, somewhere in the back of my mind, the twinkling sound of her jhumkas played on repeat, refusing to fade away.

AARNA

The past few weeks had been a blur of assignments, deadlines, and endless hours in the library, but there was something—someone—that had started to cut through the monotony. Ayaan.

I didn't know him well, not really, but there was something magnetic about him. Maybe it was the way he always had this quiet confidence, like he was in control of everything around him without ever needing to show it. Or maybe it was the way he seemed to notice little things about me—the way I'd chew on the end of my pen when I was thinking, or the way I always tucked a strand of hair behind my ear when I was focused.

Today, as I sat in the library, my mind wandered again, despite my best efforts to concentrate. Ayaan was sitting across from me, his eyes glued to his textbook, but I could feel his presence. It wasn't obvious, but it was there—a warmth, a quiet energy that seemed to pull me in.

I tried to focus on the notes in front of me, but I couldn't help it. Every now and then, my gaze would shift toward him, and I'd catch him looking back at me. Just a quick glance, but it sent a fluttering feeling through my chest every time.

And then, it happened. Ayaan casually stretched his leg under the table, and his foot brushed against mine.

I froze, unsure of what to do. The touch was so brief, so accidental—or at least it seemed that way—but my pulse quickened. I glanced up at him, only to find him watching me intently, his lips curling into a playful smile.

"I think you're staring at me," he said, his voice low, teasing.

My cheeks warmed instantly, and I quickly looked away, pretending to focus on my notes. "I'm not staring."

"Hmm," Ayaan murmured, clearly unconvinced. "I think you're lying."

I couldn't stop the small laugh that escaped me, but I didn't dare look at him again. Instead, I pushed my notes aside, feeling the sudden pressure of the moment building between us.

Without warning, Ayaan shifted closer, and his foot brushed against mine again. This time, he didn't pull away. His touch lingered, sending a shiver up my spine.

I was about to say something—anything—to break the tension, but before I could, Ayaan leaned in just slightly. His lips were near my ear, and his voice was so soft, it felt like a secret only the two of us shared.

"You know, if you keep doing that, I might think you're trying to distract me on purpose."

My heart skipped a beat. I didn't know what to say, how to respond to that. Instead, I just swallowed, trying to focus on anything other than the way his words seemed to hang in the air, between us.

But then, he pulled back, flashing me that confident, knowing grin again. "You're trouble, Aarna," he said, a hint of mischief in his tone.

I couldn't help but feel like he was right. I had no idea how we'd gone from two strangers in a library to this moment, but one thing was clear—I wasn't ready for it to end. The chemistry between us was undeniable, and the way his gaze lingered on mine made me question everything I thought I knew about control.

But I wasn't going to make it easy for him, not just yet. So, I matched his grin, leaning back in my chair as I said, "You have no idea."

And just like that, the air around us seemed to shift, leaving me wondering what would happen next.

9

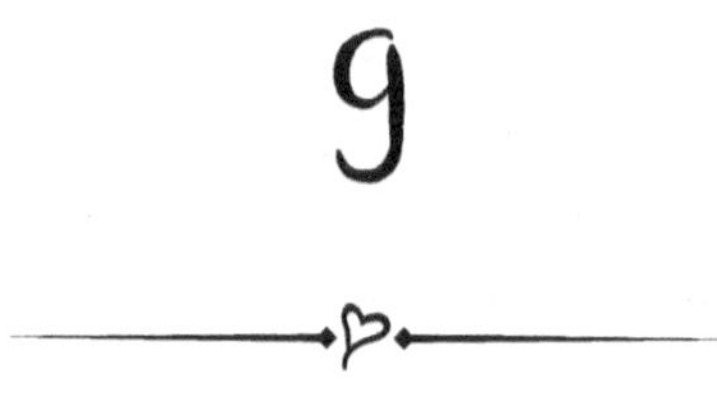

AYAAN

The library had become a strange haven for me, not because I enjoyed studying, but because it was the one place where I could always find Aarna. Today was no different. We were both buried in our work, but the quiet hum of the library, the rustle of pages, and the faint scent of old books all faded into the background as I focused on her.

Aarna wasn't your typical person. She had this way about her—calm, composed, yet there was something about her that kept me on my toes. She didn't let people get too close, but there was something in the way she looked at me when she thought I wasn't paying attention. It made my heart race in a way I didn't expect.

I glanced up from my textbook, only to find her looking at me. Her eyes were softer than usual, like she had been thinking about something, but she quickly looked away, pretending to focus on her notes. It was a subtle move, but it didn't escape me. There was something unspoken hanging between us, something neither of us was willing to acknowledge outright.

I couldn't help it. I shifted a little, moving closer to her, careful not to draw the attention of the librarian who was pacing up and down the aisles. But here, between the rows of books, it was like we were in our own world. My breath caught in my throat as I noticed how close we were, how the space between us seemed to shrink with each passing second.

A moment later, I felt the tension building—like the air itself was charged. We were facing each other now, just a few inches apart, our eyes locked in a silent exchange that spoke louder than words ever could. I could hear the steady rhythm of her breathing, and it seemed like the world outside us had faded away. The only sound was the occasional rustle of paper and the distant murmur of the librarian's footsteps.

My heart was hammering in my chest, and I could feel her presence like a pull I couldn't resist. I don't know why I did it, but without thinking, I reached out, brushing my fingers against her hand. The touch was light, tentative at first, but she didn't pull away. Instead, she hesitated, as though processing what was happening.

And then, without a word, she let her hand rest in mine.

The electricity between us was undeniable. Her fingers curled around mine, and for a brief moment, I thought the whole world had stopped. I could feel the warmth of her skin, the gentle pressure of her hand in mine. Our breath had become uneven, each of us acutely aware of the proximity, the intensity of the moment.

I could see the flicker of something in her eyes—surprise, maybe, or curiosity. Whatever it was, it made me want to hold on tighter, to make this moment last just a little longer. But the air around us was thick with anticipation, and I knew we couldn't stay like this forever, not here, not with the librarian just a few steps away.

I pulled my hand back slowly, reluctantly, but the connection between us still lingered in the space we had shared. A few seconds passed before I looked at her again, and there was a softness in her gaze that I hadn't seen before. She smiled faintly, a smile that made my heart skip a beat.

"You know," she said quietly, breaking the silence, "we should probably get back to work."

I nodded, though I wasn't sure if I could focus on anything now. But one thing was clear—I was glad Aarna hadn't listened to Kaira or the rumors. She hadn't let them shape her perception of me. And somehow, in this tiny, stolen moment, I knew that whatever this was between us, it was real.

10

AARNA

The day had been dragging on, and I was trying to focus, but my mind kept wandering. I had convinced myself that this whole situation with Ayaan wasn't something to get caught up in, but every time I tried to push it out of my head, something pulled me back in. There was a tension between us that neither of us was addressing, but it was there. I could feel it in every glance, every passing moment.

We had spent so many hours together lately—more than I had planned. But it wasn't just the proximity that got to me. It was the way he was with me, like he genuinely cared, like I wasn't just some passing acquaintance to him. And it made it so much harder to ignore the way my heart seemed to race every time he spoke or when his eyes lingered a little longer than usual.

I kept telling myself that I should focus on my studies. That I shouldn't be distracted by Ayaan or any of the nonsense that others were saying. But it wasn't as easy as I thought it would be.

We were in between classes when he walked up to me, casually leaning against the wall next to where I was standing. He didn't say anything at first, just standing there like he was waiting for me to make the first move. And for a moment, I didn't know what to say. The air felt thick, charged. His presence felt closer than it had ever been.

Finally, he spoke.

"You're avoiding me," Ayaan said, his voice low and almost teasing. "I thought we were past this."

I blinked, caught off guard. "What do you mean?"

"You know exactly what I mean," he said with a half-smile, his eyes searching mine. "I'm not some stranger you have to avoid."

For some reason, that simple statement made my heart do something funny. There was a sincerity in his voice, a softness in the way he was looking at me. And, despite everything I'd told myself, it was hard not to feel drawn to him.

I took a step back, trying to gather myself. "I'm not avoiding you," I said, but I could hear the uncertainty in my voice.

"You are," he replied, his hand brushing against mine in the most natural of gestures. It felt like it wasn't an accident, like he had meant to do it. And just like that, a spark of something lit up between us.

I didn't pull away. I couldn't. Instead, my hand rested in his, just for a moment, but it was enough to make my breath hitch. I looked up at him, his face close to mine, his expression unreadable. The world around us seemed to fade away, and for a second, I didn't care about anything else.

Ayaan's grip on my hand tightened slightly, just enough to make me feel his presence even more intensely. My heart pounded, and I couldn't tell if it was from nervousness or excitement—or both. I could feel his gaze on me, and it was as though time had slowed down.

"I'm glad you didn't listen to the rumors," he said softly, his thumb brushing the back of my hand. "It means more than you think."

For a split second, I forgot to breathe. His words hit me in a way I wasn't expecting. I had never expected someone to say something like that to me—especially not him.

"I didn't listen to them," I said, almost as if I was convincing myself as much as him. "But... I still don't know what this is."

Ayaan's eyes softened. "I don't know either," he admitted. "But I don't want to let go just yet."

It wasn't a confession, but it was something more—a promise, perhaps, or the beginning of one.

Before I could respond, he let go of my hand and took a step back, but the warmth of his touch lingered, and I couldn't shake the feeling that this moment was something I wouldn't forget anytime soon.

"I'll see you later," he said, his voice a little quieter now, almost like he was trying to give me space to process everything.

As he walked away, I stood there, my thoughts a whirlwind. I hadn't expected him to make things feel so... real. But he had, and now I couldn't escape it. Not that I wanted to.

11

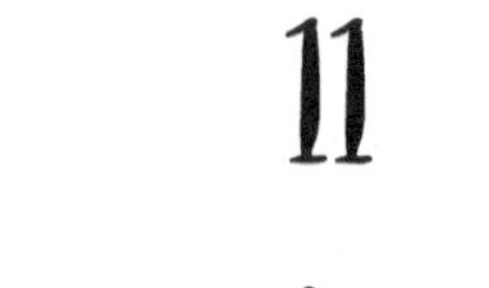

AARNA

The days that followed felt almost surreal. After everything that had happened with Ayaan—after opening up to him about my past, my trust issues, and the pain I'd been carrying for so long—it felt like a weight had been lifted off my shoulders. The air between us was different now, lighter. We were spending more time together than I ever expected, and I didn't mind it one bit. If anything, I was grateful for it.

Every conversation with Ayaan seemed to lead to something deeper, something real. It wasn't just about the assignments anymore. It was about who we were, what we wanted, and what had shaped us into the people we were today.

We met at the library a few times to work on our project, but it wasn't long before the work was pushed to the background, and we found ourselves sitting in the little coffee shop near campus, talking about everything and nothing at all. The moments we spent together felt like stolen ones, but somehow, they felt right.

"I still can't believe I'm trusting you with all of this," I said, stirring my coffee absentmindedly, watching the swirling pattern the spoon created. "I've never really told anyone about Rishi before. Not like this."

Ayaan leaned back in his chair, his eyes thoughtful as he took a sip of his coffee. "I'm glad you did. I think it's good for you. Holding that stuff in... it's not healthy."

I nodded, his words sinking in. It was hard for me to admit that, for so long, I had kept so much inside. But in Ayaan's company, it didn't feel like a burden. It felt like something I could let go of.

We'd started talking about family, about the things that mattered most to us, and what we each wanted from life. Ayaan shared his dreams of becoming successful—about how he wanted to make his parents proud. I admired how determined he was, even though he didn't always show it. He was always so confident on the outside, but I could tell there was so much more beneath the surface.

"What about you?" he asked one day, his voice low but curious. "What's your dream, Aarna?"

I hesitated, unsure if I should tell him everything. My dream seemed so far away, so complicated. But for some reason, I didn't feel scared to share it with him.

"I guess... I want to make something of myself. Not just for my parents, but for me. I've always been the good girl, the one who follows the rules, but I want to do something that makes me feel alive. Something that makes me proud."

Ayaan's gaze softened as he listened, and I could see the understanding in his eyes. He didn't interrupt or try to give me advice. He just let me speak.

"I've never really felt that freedom, you know? Not the way I want to," I continued, suddenly feeling a little vulnerable. "But maybe... maybe one day, I'll get there."

Ayaan leaned forward slightly, resting his chin on his hand, his elbow propped up on the table. "You will, Aarna. I believe in you. You're stronger than you think."

His words wrapped around me like a warm blanket, and for the first time in a long while, I believed him. I had spent so many years doubting myself, thinking I wasn't capable of being anything more than the good, dependable daughter. But Ayaan made me feel like there was more to me than I had given myself credit for.

The next few days blurred together, filled with late-night study sessions, spontaneous outings, and random moments of conversation. One evening, after finishing up our assignment at his place, we went for a walk along the nearby park. It was a quiet night, the air cool but not too chilly. The stars hung above us, barely visible through the city's lights, but still managing to shine through.

"I'm glad we're doing this," Ayaan said, his voice breaking the silence. "Spending time together, I mean. I didn't think I'd be this comfortable with someone in such a short amount of time."

I looked up at him, surprised by the honesty in his words. "Yeah, me neither. I guess it's just easy with you. It doesn't feel forced."

He smiled, the kind of smile that made his eyes light up. "I'm glad to hear that."

As we walked, we kept talking, our conversation flowing without effort. We talked about everything—our childhoods, our favorite memories, our hopes for the future. It felt like we were unraveling each other bit by bit, learning things we hadn't known before.

But it wasn't just the deep conversations that had me falling for him. It was the small, almost imperceptible moments—the way he made sure I always had my jacket when the air turned colder, the way his hand brushed against mine when we were walking side by side, the way his smile would brighten when he saw me laugh. Those moments made my heart race, and for once, I didn't mind it.

"You know," Ayaan said, his voice breaking through my thoughts, "I never expected us to get this close. It just kind of happened."

I chuckled softly, looking up at him. "Yeah, I didn't expect it either. But here we are."

He stopped walking and turned to face me, his expression suddenly serious. "I'm glad it did, Aarna. I really am. You're... you're different from anyone I've ever met. And I'm not just saying that because you're the one I'm working with on a project."

I felt my heart skip a beat, but I didn't want to make it awkward. "I'm glad we crossed paths too," I said, my voice soft.

His gaze lingered on mine, and for a second, I thought he might say something else. But he didn't. Instead, he reached for my hand, taking it gently in his. "Let's not overthink it. Let's just enjoy this."

I nodded, feeling a warmth spread through my chest. It was exactly what I needed to hear. There was no rush, no pressure. We were just two people who had found each other, and for the first time in a long while, I felt like everything was exactly as it should be.

And with that, we continued walking, hand in hand, toward whatever came next.

ᑭᑭᑭ

The evening air was cool, and Ayaan and I had been walking for what felt like hours, lost in conversation and laughter. It was the kind of night that made everything feel right, and for once, I didn't feel like the world was closing in on me.

We walked past a little café near the corner, and Ayaan suggested we stop for a quick drink. "Let's grab something to warm us up. I'm feeling a hot chocolate," he said, giving me a playful look.

"Hot chocolate sounds perfect," I replied, smiling as we made our way inside.

The café was cozy, with soft lighting and the comforting scent of freshly brewed coffee in the air. We made our way to the counter to place our orders, talking about how we had both managed to survive a long week of assignments and deadlines.

As I was reaching into my bag for my wallet, I felt a familiar presence behind me. I turned around, and my heart nearly stopped when I saw him—Rishi.

His eyes were fixed on us, his gaze flicking from Ayaan's hand in mine to my face, then back again. There was an unmistakable look of surprise, mixed with something else—something I couldn't quite place. It was like he was caught off guard, his expression softening for a moment before his usual guardedness took over.

I felt my face go pale, and I instinctively pulled my hand away from Ayaan's, stepping back slightly. My heart started to race, and for a moment, I forgot how to breathe.

Ayaan noticed the shift in my demeanor immediately. He looked over his shoulder, seeing Rishi standing there, and then back at me. He didn't say anything, but I could feel his grip on the situation—on me—tighten, like he was silently telling me everything would be okay.

"Hey, Aarna," Rishi said, his voice a little quieter than usual, his eyes still locked on our hands. He didn't seem mad or jealous, but there was something off in his expression, like he was processing a lot all at once.

"Hi, Rishi," I replied, my voice barely above a whisper. My pulse was pounding in my ears. I felt suddenly small, exposed, as if the weight of everything between us was pressing down on me.

Rishi's gaze lingered on Ayaan for a beat longer than it should've, and then he shifted his attention back to me. He opened his mouth to say something, but it seemed like words failed him. Instead, he gave a tight nod and half-smiled, his eyes flickering with a mix of confusion and something else I couldn't quite decipher.

"Well, I'll see you around, Aarna," Rishi said after a beat, his tone polite but distant. He didn't acknowledge Ayaan directly but gave him a quick glance before turning and heading out of the café.

I let out a breath I hadn't realized I was holding, but my chest still felt tight. The moment felt like it had stretched on for too long, and I couldn't shake the unease that settled over me. Rishi's presence, his look, it all felt so... heavy. It reminded me of everything I had tried to bury, everything I had moved on from, but still hadn't fully let go of.

Ayaan stood there quietly, watching me. His hand, which I had instinctively pulled away from, now hovered close, as though unsure whether to reach out for me again.

"You okay?" he asked softly, his voice laced with concern.

I nodded quickly, though it didn't feel like the truth. "Yeah, I'm fine. Just... caught off guard."

"I could tell," he said, stepping closer to me. "If you want to talk about it, I'm here, Aarna. But I get it if you don't."

I felt a wave of gratitude toward him, toward how understanding he was, even though he didn't know the full depth of what I was feeling in that moment. "Thanks, Ayaan," I murmured, giving him a small smile.

He gave me a gentle smile in return, but there was a touch of uncertainty in his eyes. "You know, I didn't mean to make things weird. I just... I didn't think it would affect you like that."

I sighed and took a deep breath, trying to steady myself. "It's not your fault. It's just... seeing him again after all this time, especially like that—it brought up a lot of old feelings."

Ayaan didn't push me to explain further. Instead, he simply reached for my hand, a small but reassuring gesture, and we moved on to grab our drinks, the weight of the moment slowly dissipating, even though the sting of Rishi's gaze lingered in my chest.

I wasn't ready to confront the reality of what had just happened, but I was grateful that, for the first time in a long while, I wasn't facing it alone.

12

AYAAN

It had been a few days since the encounter with Rishi at the café. Although the initial tension between us had settled, I couldn't ignore the undercurrent of unease that seemed to linger between Aarna and me whenever Rishi's name came up. I wasn't sure if it was because of the history they shared or something else, but it always seemed like there was a thread connecting them that I couldn't touch. I tried my best not to let it bother me, but the unease remained, just under the surface.

I had my own issues to deal with, especially as I adjusted to the busy routine at college. But nothing could quite prepare me for the moment when I walked into the campus that day and saw him—Rishi—standing at the entrance of our building. He was just there, looking casual as always, his usual confident self. But what hit me like a ton of bricks was something I hadn't expected.

Rishi was in our college.

I froze for a second, my heart skipping. I looked over at his uniform and saw that familiar name tag, this time not the one for his previous college but for St. Clair's College. My mind raced. I knew he wasn't in the same program as me. Aarna had always been in the commerce department, and I was in economics, but now, seeing Rishi here... it only meant one thing.

He had transferred in.

I didn't know how or why, but there he was, in the same college. In my college.

I swallowed the lump in my throat as I stood there, trying to process the unexpected blow to my calm. I told myself to breathe, to keep my composure. It wasn't like I had any reason to be worried, right? Aarna and I were just figuring things out. We weren't even officially anything yet. But still... there was this irrational fear growing inside me, one I couldn't shake.

I tried to keep my focus as I walked into the building, but my eyes kept darting back to Rishi. He hadn't noticed me yet. He was talking to some of the other students, laughing as if it was all normal. But something about it felt off—like a warning bell ringing in my head.

And then it hit me: Aarna and Rishi would be seeing each other in class, in the same place, probably working on group projects together. That terrified me more than I wanted to admit.

I couldn't concentrate the rest of the day. It was all I could think about. I could feel the gnawing jealousy growing in the pit of my stomach, even though I tried to rationalize it. I didn't know what it was, but seeing him here, in our space, made me feel like I was losing my grip on something important.

After class, I lingered in the hallway, watching as Aarna walked out of the lecture room with her friends. My heart lurched when I saw Rishi approach her, and they stood there, talking, laughing like they always did. Her face lit up as she smiled at something he said, and for a split second, I felt this pang of something dark and tight in my chest.

I didn't know what I was scared of—maybe I was afraid of losing her to him. I couldn't deny it anymore. My feelings for Aarna were growing stronger by the day, but Rishi, with his history with her, was like this looming shadow I couldn't escape.

I hated how quickly the jealousy rose in me, but I couldn't help it. I had to find a way to get closer to Aarna, to show her that I was someone worth choosing. But the fear of losing her to someone else, someone like Rishi, made my heart race with anxiety.

She didn't deserve to be in the middle of this mess. But neither did I.

I just hoped she saw me for who I was—Ayaan. Not just someone who had come after Rishi, but someone who could stand by her side and be the kind of guy she needed.

But until then, I couldn't help but worry.

13

AARNA

I didn't want to go. Every fiber of my being screamed at me to come up with an excuse, any excuse, but there was none that my mother would buy. The moment she mentioned that we had been invited to Rishi's place for his housewarming, I knew there was no getting out of it.

"It would look so bad if you don't come," Mom had said while getting ready. "We've known their family for years. Just be civil, Aarna."

Civil. Right. As if that was so easy.

So here I was, standing outside Rishi's newly furnished apartment, my arms crossed tightly over my chest as I forced a polite smile. The place was impressive, with warm-toned interiors and floor-to-ceiling windows that overlooked the city. His parents were greeting guests, and his mother practically pulled me into a hug the moment I stepped in.

"Aarna, beta! Look at you, all grown up! It's been so long since we had you over," she gushed, her warmth genuine despite the awkwardness I felt. I forced a small smile and nodded, scanning the room.

And then, as if he could sense me, Rishi appeared.

I wished I could say my heart didn't skip a beat when I saw him again, but that would be a lie. He was standing there in a casual dark blue shirt, his hands stuffed in his pockets, looking at me with an expression I couldn't quite decipher.

"Aarna," he said, a small smirk tugging at his lips. "Didn't think you'd actually show up."

"Trust me, neither did I," I muttered under my breath, just enough for him to hear. He chuckled, clearly amused.

My younger sister, Kaina, was already off somewhere taking pictures for Instagram. She lived for these social gatherings, unlike me. I just wanted to get this over with.

I stuck to the corner, only engaging in conversation when absolutely necessary. But of course, Rishi just had to find his way back to me.

"So," he started casually, leaning against the kitchen counter beside me. "I heard you've been spending a lot of time with Ayaan."

I stiffened. "And?"

His smirk didn't falter. "Nothing. Just... didn't peg you to be his type."

My fingers curled around the glass in my hand. His type? What the hell did that even mean?

"And what exactly is 'his type,' Rishi?" I shot back, raising a brow.

He shrugged, playing it cool. "Not you."

I scoffed, shaking my head. "Right. Because you're the expert on who I am?"

Rishi leaned in slightly, lowering his voice. "I just don't get it, Aarna. Him?"

I turned fully to face him, my eyes locking onto his. "Well, I do. And that's all that matters."

His smirk faltered for just a second, but it was enough. Enough to tell me that something about this bothered him. Good. Let him feel a fraction of what I went through when he chose someone else over me.

Just when I thought this conversation was over, he surprised me. "Come with me for a second," he said, his voice softer now.

I hesitated. "Why?"

"Just... come."

Against my better judgment, I followed him down the hall. He pushed open a door, stepping aside so I could enter first.

The moment I walked in, my breath hitched.

His room was warm, cozy—nothing like the sleek, cold bachelor pad I had expected. There were bookshelves filled with familiar titles, a soft throw blanket draped over the armchair in the corner, and his walls...

I turned, my heart stopping for a moment.

On one side of the room, a series of paintings were hung up—portraits. Of me.

My throat went dry as I took slow steps forward, my fingers brushing over one of them. Some were unfinished sketches, while others were full-blown paintings capturing me in ways I never thought someone saw me.

"You... kept these?" I whispered, unable to look at him.

"I never stopped painting you," Rishi admitted, his voice barely above a murmur.

I swallowed hard, my emotions tangled in ways I couldn't unravel. I wanted to say something, but the words wouldn't come out.

Before I could react further, my phone buzzed in my hand. I looked down, and my heart dropped.

Ayaan: You at Rishi's place?

I sucked in a breath. Kaina had posted those pictures, and now Ayaan knew.

14

AYAAN

The moment I saw Kaina's Instagram story, my blood boiled.

Rishi's housewarming. Aarna was there.

And not just as a guest standing in a corner, avoiding attention—no. The picture Kaina had posted showed her inside his place, a soft smile on her lips as she talked to his parents. She looked like she belonged there, like she was a part of his world.

My jaw clenched. I gripped my phone so tightly that my knuckles turned white.

She hadn't told me. She hadn't even mentioned it.

I wasn't supposed to care this much. I wasn't supposed to feel this rage clawing at my chest. But I did. And it was all because of him.

Rishi.

I barely knew him, yet I hated him. And I hated that he had any kind of hold over her.

I tried to push down the jealousy, the possessiveness creeping into my veins. It wasn't like Aarna was mine—but damn it, I wanted her to be.

Before I knew it, I was already dialing her number.

It rang once. Twice.

Then she picked up. "Hello?"

"Are you at his place?" My voice came out sharp, demanding.

There was silence on the other end.

"Aarna."

"…Yeah," she finally admitted, her voice small.

I exhaled harshly, running a hand through my hair. "And you weren't going to tell me?"

"Ayaan, I—"

"Forget it," I cut her off. "Enjoy your evening with him." I hung up before she could say another word.

But that didn't help. It didn't make me feel better. If anything, it made me feel worse.

I tossed my phone onto my desk, pacing my room as the anger twisted inside me. I tried to be rational. I tried to tell myself that she had her reasons, that maybe she didn't want to be there in the first place.

But then another thought hit me like a gut punch.

What if she still had feelings for him?

What if no matter what I did—no matter how close we got, how much I cared for her—I would always be second to him?

15

AARNA

I stared at my phone, rereading Ayaan's last words before he hung up.

"Enjoy your evening with him."

The sharpness in his voice lingered in my mind. It wasn't just irritation—it was something deeper. Something that made my heart squeeze uncomfortably.

I should have told him about coming here. Maybe then he wouldn't have been this mad.

But then there was Rishi.

His room. His paintings.

The moment I stepped inside, my breath had caught in my throat. Each canvas was a memory, a frozen piece of the past I thought we had buried. He had painted me—not just once, but over and over again. Different versions of me. Smiling, lost in thought, looking away, looking at him.

My chest felt tight. How was I supposed to react to that? How was I supposed to feel?

I needed a distraction. I needed my girls.

So I texted the group chat:

Aarna: Girls' night at my place. Urgent.

Simie replied almost instantly. OMG YES. What happened?

Anu: If this is about a certain someone whose name starts with A, I'm bringing popcorn.

Saniya: On my way.

I sighed. I needed their advice, but more than that, I needed to breathe.

A few hours later, we were curled up in my room, snacks spread out between us. Fairy lights glowed softly against the walls, giving the space a warm, cozy feel.

"So," Simie started, popping a chip into her mouth. "Spill."

I hesitated for a moment before exhaling. "It's about Ayaan. And... Rishi."

Anu smirked. "Love triangle alert."

I shot her a glare, but Saniya nudged me. "Start from the beginning."

So I did. I told them everything—how Ayaan had comforted me during my panic attack, how he made me pasta, how he held me when I broke down. How he called me Sunshine just to annoy me.

And then, I told them about Rishi.

About the paintings. About the way his room felt too familiar—too much like a home we had once shared.

For a moment, no one spoke.

Then Simie whistled. "Damn."

Anu leaned in, eyes twinkling. "Okay, but how do you feel?"

"I don't know," I admitted. "It's like... I'm not the same girl who loved Rishi. But seeing those paintings—it still affected me. And then there's Ayaan. He's—"

"Hot," Saniya supplied helpfully.

I rolled my eyes. "He's been there for me. In a way I never thought someone would be after everything with Rishi."

Simie tilted her head. "But?"

I chewed on my lip. "But I don't know if I can trust myself to fall for someone again. I don't know if I should."

Saniya crossed her arms. "Let me ask you one thing. If Ayaan had been at that housewarming, standing next to you, would you still have felt something when you saw those paintings?"

The question hit harder than I expected.

Would I?

I swallowed, my heart hammering in my chest.

I didn't have an answer.

ᐅᐅᐅ

Confusion.

It had settled into my chest like an unwanted guest, refusing to leave no matter how much I tried to push it away.

I had spent the entire night replaying my conversation with the girls, tossing and turning in bed as my mind raced between memories of Rishi and moments with Ayaan.

But when the morning sunlight streamed through my curtains, I made a decision.

I couldn't let this consume me.

I had bigger things to focus on—things that actually mattered.

My entrance exams were coming up, and I hadn't been as focused as I should have been. The last thing I needed was to get tangled in feelings that I wasn't even sure I understood.

So, I pulled my hair into a bun, grabbed my notes, and forced myself into study mode.

By noon, I was sitting at my usual spot in the library, highlighters and textbooks spread out around me.

I had just started solving a mock test when my phone buzzed.

Ayaan: You free?

I stared at the message.

A part of me wanted to say yes. To call him, hear his voice, pretend everything was normal. But then I remembered the way he spoke to me last night when he found out I was at Rishi's house. The way his voice had held something dangerously close to hurt.

I shook my head and typed back:

Me: Not today. Need to study.

A few seconds later, the typing bubbles appeared.

Ayaan: Alright, nerd. Don't forget to eat.

I exhaled, a small smile tugging at my lips. But I quickly shook it off.

Focus, Aarna.

I switched off my phone, flipped the page of my textbook, and forced myself to drown in numbers and logic.

Maybe if I kept myself busy enough, my heart would stop feeling so damn conflicted.

16

AYAAN

For the first time in weeks, I decided to shut everything else out and just focus.

No distractions. No unnecessary thoughts.

Just me and my CA entrance prep.

I had wasted enough time already—time spent overthinking, trying to decode my own feelings, and worrying about things that weren't in my control. But not anymore.

If Aarna could zone in on her studies, so could I.

I sat at my desk, my notes sprawled out in front of me, and took a deep breath. The syllabus was massive, but I had to tackle it piece by piece.

The first hour went smoothly—solving accounts felt like second nature, and for once, my brain wasn't running in circles around a certain someone.

But then my phone buzzed.

For a second, I thought about checking it. A small part of me hoped it was her. But then I clenched my jaw, flipped my phone over, and went back to my textbook.

I wasn't going to let anything—or anyone—distract me.

Not now.

Not when I had worked this hard to get here.

Aarna and whatever this thing between us was could wait. But my future? That couldn't.

51

17

AARNA

The world outside my window blurred into an unrecognizable mess of streetlights and city noise, but none of it mattered. My head was buried in notes, my fingers tapping against the highlighted sections in my book as I repeated concepts under my breath.

For weeks now, my life had been reduced to one thing—study, eat, sleep, repeat.

I had taken a break from college, skipped unnecessary outings, and barely looked at my phone except for study-related conversations. Simie and Anu had started calling me a nerd in hibernation, and honestly? They weren't wrong.

The CA entrance was right around the corner, and nothing—not even my own spiraling thoughts—was going to distract me.

Except maybe Ayaan.

"Wait, repeat that?" I asked, rubbing my temples as I leaned back against my chair.

Ayaan sighed through the phone. "I said, in company law, the doctrine of indoor management—"

"—protects outsiders dealing with a company in good faith," I finished for him. "They aren't expected to know the internal irregularities that might exist within the company."

A soft chuckle came from the other end. "Look at you, sunshine. Already answering before I finish."

I rolled my eyes at the nickname, but before I could reply, the doorbell rang.

Frowning, I placed my phone on speaker and got up. It was almost midnight—who could possibly be here at this hour?

When I opened the door, my breath hitched.

"Hey," Rishi said, standing there with a small smile and a tub of ice cream in his hands. "Thought you could use a break."

For a second, I just stared at him. The familiarity of it all—the way he casually walked into my space like he still belonged here—made my stomach churn.

"Aarna?" Ayaan's voice crackled through the phone, reminding me he was still on the line.

I snapped out of my daze. "Uh—Rishi's here. I'll call you back, okay?"

There was a pause. Ayaan didn't say anything for a moment, but when he did, his voice was unreadable.

"Yeah. Sure."

I ended the call, placing my phone on the table as I turned back to Rishi.

"Come on in," I muttered, stepping aside.

We sat on the couch, the dim glow of the lamp casting soft shadows in the room. Rishi handed me a spoon, and I took a bite of the ice cream, the cold sweetness melting against my tongue.

"So, how's studying going?" he asked, leaning back comfortably.

I sighed dramatically. "It's brutal. If I stare at another business law section, I might actually cry."

Rishi chuckled. "I can imagine. You were always the overachiever."

I shot him a glare. "Excuse me for having a plan."

He smirked. "Right, right. Aarna-the-planner."

I rolled my eyes, but a laugh bubbled out anyway. It was easy, natural—the kind of comfort I hadn't felt in a long time.

Rishi watched me for a second, something soft flickering in his gaze. Then, before I could react, he reached forward and tucked a loose strand of hair behind my ear. His fingers lingered for a moment, his touch light but deliberate.

"I missed this," he murmured, his voice barely above a whisper.

Something in my chest tightened. The air shifted between us, heavy with unspoken words, unfinished endings.

I swallowed, my voice just as quiet.

"So did I."

18

AYAAN

The classroom was buzzing with the usual pre-exam tension. Papers shuffled, whispered discussions filled the air, and the professor was already handing out the mock question papers at the front of the room.

I tapped my pen against the desk, my knee bouncing slightly as I glanced at the empty seat beside me.

Where the hell was Aarna?

She never missed a mock exam. Never.

Frowning, I pulled out my phone and dialed her number. It rang for a few seconds before I finally heard her groggy, sleep-filled voice.

"Hello?"

I blinked. Was she still asleep?

"Aarna?" I hissed under my breath, lowering my voice so the professor wouldn't hear me. "Where are you? The business law mock already started!"

There was a sharp intake of breath, followed by a series of rustling noises on her end.

"Shit," she mumbled. "I—I fell asleep. I was talking to Rishi and—I forgot to set an alarm—"

My grip on the pen tightened.

Of course. Rishi.

I exhaled through my nose, forcing my voice to stay calm. "Okay, just get here fast. I'll tell sir you got stuck in traffic or something."

"I'll be there in five minutes! Just stall him, please."

Before I could say anything else, she hung up.

I clenched my jaw, shoving my phone back into my bag. A weird knot twisted in my stomach, but I pushed it aside. This wasn't the time. Right now, she needed a cover, and as much as I hated the reason for her being late, I wasn't about to let her miss this exam.

Taking a deep breath, I raised my hand.

"Sir?" I called out, putting on my most convincing expression. "Aarna got stuck in traffic. She's on the way."

The professor sighed, checking his watch before nodding. "Fine, but if she's not here in the next five minutes, she's not writing this exam."

I gave a curt nod, even as my jaw clenched.

Five minutes.

For the first time since I'd known Aarna, I wondered if she would really make it.

19

AARNA

I had never gotten ready this fast in my life.

One second, I was deep in sleep, tangled in my blanket, and the next, I was shoving my feet into my sneakers, grabbing my books, and running out the door.

I didn't even have time to process how I'd fallen asleep mid-conversation with Rishi last night.

I had forgotten to set an alarm. Me.

The same person who planned everything to the last detail, who never missed a study session, who never showed up late to an exam.

God, Ayaan was going to kill me.

I reached the exam hall, breathless, my hair barely tied up in a messy bun. My heart was still racing as I spotted Ayaan sitting in his seat, arms crossed, looking straight ahead.

I could tell he was mad.

I didn't have time to deal with that now.

"S-Sir, I'm here," I stammered, handing over my ID.

The professor barely looked up as he gestured toward my seat. "You have exactly one hour left. No extra time."

I nodded, quickly slipping into my chair. My hands were still shaking as I picked up my pen and flipped over the paper. Focus, Aarna.

But I could feel Ayaan's stare on me.

I swallowed, not daring to meet his eyes.

I knew exactly what he was thinking./

20

AYAAN

I waited until the mock exam was over.

The moment Aarna stepped out of the exam hall, I grabbed her wrist, pulling her aside before she could escape.

"What the hell was that?" My voice was lower than usual, controlled—but barely.

She blinked up at me, confused. "What?"

"You missed the exam, Aarna. You. The most disciplined, most planned-out person I know. And why? Because you fell asleep talking to him?"

Her lips parted as if to protest, but she stopped. She knew I wasn't wrong.

I exhaled sharply, running a hand through my hair. "I need to know where we stand, Aarna. I can't do this anymore."

Her brows furrowed. "Do what?"

"This... thing between us. You spend time with me, let me hold you, open up to me in ways I know you don't with anyone else. But then he shows up, and suddenly, it's like I don't exist."

"Ayaan, it's not like that—"

"Then tell me what it is."

She was silent.

I clenched my jaw, my voice dropping. "I like you, Aarna. More than I should. And I thought—" I shook my head. "It doesn't matter what I thought. What matters is that you need to choose."

Her eyes widened.

"Rishi or me."

Her breath hitched, but I continued.

"I won't be your second option. I won't be the person you run to when he's not around." My throat felt tight, but I pushed through. "So figure it out, Aarna. Because I swear, if you choose him, I'll walk away. And this time, I won't look back."

I let go of her wrist, stepping back.

Just as I turned to walk away, something snapped inside me, and I spun back around. My voice was sharp, almost bitter.

"And one more thing—how the hell could you sleep with your ex?"

Aarna's eyes flashed with something between shock and anger. "Stop making it sound like we did something," she snapped. "We didn't. We just—fell asleep next to each other. That's it."

I let out a hollow laugh. "Right. Because that makes it so much better."

"Ayaan—"

I shook my head. "Forget it."

I turned around and walked away. Because if I stayed a second longer, I knew I'd say something I couldn't take back.

21

AARNA

The weight of the final exam lifted as I handed in my paper, a wave of relief washing over me. Weeks of relentless study had culminated in this moment, and the promise of freedom beckoned.

To celebrate, my friends—Kaira, Somya, Anu, Sahir, and about ten others—proposed a getaway to my family's villa in Lonavala. The idea was met with unanimous excitement; we all craved a break from the academic grind.

Nestled amidst the lush greenery of Lonavala, our villa was a sanctuary of tranquility. The two-story structure boasted spacious rooms adorned with large windows that invited the serene beauty of the surrounding landscape inside. The living area opened up to a sprawling backyard, where a pristine swimming pool glistened under the sun. Tall palm trees swayed gently around the pool, casting dappled shadows on the water's surface. A wooden deck with lounge chairs bordered the pool, providing the perfect spot for sunbathing or stargazing at night.

Upon arrival, the villa buzzed with our collective excitement. Bags were hastily dropped in rooms as everyone gathered in the living area.

"This place is amazing, Aarna!" Kaira exclaimed, her eyes wide as she took in the high ceilings and tasteful decor.

"Wait until you see the pool," I replied with a grin.

Sahir peeked through the glass doors leading to the backyard. "I call dibs on the biggest float!"

Laughter erupted as we changed into swimwear and headed outside. The sun was warm, and the clear blue water of the pool was too inviting to resist.

"Cannonball!" Sahir shouted, leaping into the pool and sending a cascade of water over those of us at the edge.

"Sahir!" Somya squealed, wiping water from her face.

"You're going to pay for that," Anu warned, a mischievous glint in her eye as she slid into the water.

A playful water fight ensued, with splashes and laughter filling the air. We formed teams, attempting to dunk each other, the cool water a refreshing contrast to the sun's heat.

After exhausting ourselves, we lounged on the deck, soaking in the sun. Kaira strummed a guitar she had brought along, her fingers dancing over the strings.

"Any requests?" she asked, looking around.

"Play that song we all love," Somya suggested.

Kaira nodded and began playing, her voice harmonizing with the gentle strumming. We joined in, our voices melding together, creating a melody that resonated with our shared memories.

As dusk settled, we gathered in the living room for games. Anu set up a board game on the coffee table.

"Prepare to be defeated," she declared confidently.

"Big talk for someone who always loses," Sahir teased.

"This time will be different," Anu shot back, narrowing her eyes playfully.

The game was filled with friendly banter and competitive spirit. Sahir's quick wit kept us laughing, while

Kaira's strategic moves had us on our toes.

Later, Somya suggested a karaoke session. We took turns selecting songs, some delivering impressive performances, others delightfully off-key.

"I didn't know you could sing like that!" I exclaimed after Somya's soulful rendition of a classic ballad.

"There's a lot you don't know about me," she replied with a wink.

When it was my turn, I chose an upbeat pop song. Halfway through, I forgot the lyrics, and we all dissolved into laughter.

As the night deepened, we moved outside to the deck, the sky a canvas of stars above us. We lay on the lounge chairs, sharing stories and dreams, the bond between us growing stronger with each passing moment.

Despite Ayaan's absence due to prior commitments, the trip was a much-needed escape. It reminded me of the importance of cherishing moments of happiness and the value of surrounding oneself with supportive and loving friends.

As I lay in bed that night, the sounds of my friends' laughter still echoing in my ears, I felt a profound sense of contentment. The villa, with its comforting embrace, had provided the perfect setting for our post-exam celebration, and I was grateful for the memories we had created together.

22

❦

AYAAN

The days felt unusually long without Aarna around. Her absence was a void I couldn't ignore, and I found myself constantly checking my phone, hoping for a message or a call. The realization hit me hard: I missed her more than I cared to admit.

Unable to bear the silence any longer, I decided to reach out. I typed out a message:

"Hey Aarna, hope you're doing well. Would you like to catch up at Rising Cafe near classes once you're back?"

After a few moments, my phone buzzed with her reply:

"a smiley face"

The simple smiley face was enough to lift my spirits. I resolved that when we met, I would keep my emotions in check and have an open, honest conversation with her about everything that had been weighing on my mind.

The anticipation of seeing her again filled me with a mix of excitement and nervousness. I knew this conversation was crucial, and I was determined to approach it with patience and understanding.

23

AARNA

After returning from the refreshing trip to Lonavala, I felt a renewed sense of energy. Eager to reconnect with my close friend Jai, I decided to surprise him with a visit. Knowing our shared love for street food, especially pani puri, I called him up.

"Kem cho, Jai?" (how are you Jai) I greeted him cheerfully.

"Majama chu. Tame kem cho?" (Im good, how are you) he responded, his voice filled with pleasant surprise.

"Hu pan majama chu. Tari yaad aavi, etle vicharyu ke mali laisu." (im good too, i was remembering you so thought to meet you)

We decided to meet at the famous pani puri stall near his place. As I approached the stall, I spotted Jai waiting, his face lighting up as he saw me.

"Aarna! It's been so long since we last met."

"I know, right? Feels like ages."

We ordered our plates and began catching up between bites.

"How was your trip?" he inquired.

"It was great! Had a lot of fun with friends."

"That's awesome. What all did you guys do there?"

"Swimming, games, karaoke... a lot of things."

"Karaoke? I bet you sang your heart out!" he teased.

"Oh, stop it. Remember how many times I tried singing back in school?"

"Yeah, and I was always there to listen to your endless tales."

We both laughed, reminiscing about our school days. The pani puri vendor handed us our plates, and we continued our conversation.

"So, what's been up with you lately?" he asked.

"Just got some free time after exams."

"That's good. So, any plans for tonight?"

"Nothing much. Do you have any plans?"

"How about we catch a movie?"

"Sounds like a great idea. What time?"

"How about 7 PM?"

"Perfect. I'll be there."

As we finalized our plans, I realized how much I had missed these simple moments with Jai. Our friendship was effortless, filled with shared memories and an understanding that didn't require words. The evening promised more laughter and nostalgia, and I looked forward to every moment of it.

ᗱᗱᗱ

After the movie, Jai and I headed to my favorite Chinese restaurant, a cozy spot known for its dim lighting and authentic flavors. As we settled into our booth, the aroma of sizzling dishes filled the air, making my mouth water.

"So, what's been on your mind lately?" Jai asked, his eyes reflecting genuine concern.

I took a deep breath, gathering my thoughts. "There's something I need to talk to you about."

"Go on, I'm all ears."

"It's about Ayaan and Rishi."

Jai raised an eyebrow, intrigued. "Oh? What's going on with them?"

"Well, Ayaan confessed his feelings for me and asked me to choose between him and Rishi."

"Wow, that's quite a situation. How do you feel about them?"

"I'm confused. Ayaan has been supportive, especially during our exam preparations. But Rishi... we've shared so much history."

Jai leaned back, contemplating. "It's not an easy decision."

"Exactly. I don't want to hurt either of them, but I also need to be true to myself."

Just then, the waiter arrived to take our order.

The Hakka noodles were a delightful medley of thin, stir-fried noodles tossed with crisp bell peppers, and cabbage, all imbued with a savory soy-based sauce. The fried rice was equally enticing, featuring perfectly cooked grains mixed with peas, corn, and finely chopped green beans, offering a subtle yet satisfying flavor. The highlight was the chili Manchurian: succulent vegetable balls made from grated cabbage, deep-fried to a golden brown, and then simmered in a tangy, spicy sauce that had just the right amount of heat.

As we savored the meal, the conversation continued.

Jai smirked playfully. "You know, you won't find a guy as good as me."

I chuckled, shaking my head. "You're my best friend, Jai. We're beyond all that."

"I know, just trying to lighten the mood." He smiled warmly. "On a serious note, think about who makes you feel more like yourself. Who brings out the best in you?"

I nodded, absorbing his words. "That's good advice."

"And remember, it's your happiness that matters most. Don't rush the decision. Take your time to figure out what's right for you."

"Thanks, Jai. I appreciate your support."

"Anytime. Now, let's order before I start eating the table."

We both laughed, the tension easing as we delved into the menu, the weight of the conversation lifting slightly.

24

AYAAN

As I sat at our usual corner table in The Rising Café, my mind raced with thoughts of Aarna. The aroma of freshly brewed coffee filled the air, mingling with the soft hum of conversations around me. I glanced at my watch, noting that it was a few minutes past our agreed meeting time. Just then, the bell above the door chimed, and I looked up to see Aarna walking in.

She wore a blue tank top that complemented her complexion, paired with fitted jeans that accentuated her slender frame. Her hair cascaded freely over her shoulders, and the silver hoops she wore glinted softly under the café's warm lighting. A subtle sheen of lip balm highlighted her smile as she spotted me and made her way over.

"Hey, Ayaan!" she greeted, her voice bright.

"Hey, Aarna. You look great."

"Thanks!" she replied, taking a seat across from me. "It's been a while."

"Yeah, it has. How were your exams?"

"They went well, I think."

"That's good to hear. And your trip to Lonavala?"

"Oh, it was amazing!"

"Sounds like you had a blast."

"Yeah, it was a much-needed break after the exams."

I nodded, taking a sip of my coffee. The conversation flowed easily, but there was an underlying tension I couldn't ignore. I knew I had to address the topic that had been weighing on my mind.

"Aarna, there's something I need to talk to you about."

"Sure, what's up?"

"It's about Rishi."

Her expression shifted slightly, a hint of apprehension in her eyes.

"What about him?"

"I know you two have a history, and I respect that. But I need to know where we stand."

"Ayaan, I..."

"I care about you a lot, Aarna. And I need to know if there's a chance for us."

She looked down, her fingers tracing the rim of her coffee cup.

"I don't want to hurt anyone, Ayaan."

"I understand. But I need to know how you feel."

She sighed, meeting my gaze.

"I care about you too, Ayaan. But I need time to figure things out."

"Take all the time you need. I'll be here."

The conversation hung in the air, heavy with unspoken emotions. We sat in silence for a moment, the clinking of cups and murmur of voices around us fading into the background.

"Thank you for understanding, Ayaan."

"Of course, Aarna. I just want you to be happy."

She smiled softly, and for a moment, the tension eased. We continued our conversation, steering towards lighter topics, but the weight of our discussion lingered, a reminder of the complexities of our relationship.

25

AARNA

The early morning sun cast golden hues across the sky as we arrived at the farmhouse, a serene getaway nestled in the outskirts of the city. The vast estate stretched before us, boasting lush green gardens, a pristine swimming pool, and a cozy wooden cottage that blended seamlessly with the natural beauty surrounding it. The air was crisp, carrying the scent of fresh earth and blooming flowers, setting the perfect mood for a break from our rigorous studies.

I had opted for a comfortable yet chic outfit—a white crop top paired with denim shorts, my hair tied in a high ponytail, and my signature silver hoops adorning my ears. The moment we arrived, we wasted no time in exploring the place. Some settled on the patio, while others ran towards the poolside. Laughter and chatter filled the air as everyone basked in the carefree atmosphere.

Ayaan stepped out of the cottage in his swim trunks, looking effortlessly attractive. His toned physique and confident demeanor didn't go unnoticed by me, and I quickly averted my gaze before anyone caught me staring. We soon divided into teams for a friendly game of volleyball by the pool. Ayaan and I ended up on opposing teams, and the competitive energy between us was undeniable. Every time he scored a point, he smirked at me, making me roll my eyes and hit back with equal determination.

After an intense game filled with dives, splashes, and playful banter, we took a break by the poolside. Just as I was reaching for my bottle of lemonade, my phone vibrated. It was a missed call from Krishna.

With a teasing smile, I muttered, "Watch, he must have called to tell me results are out."

Somya, who was scrolling through her phone nearby, suddenly gasped. "OH MY GOD! The results are actually out!"

The cheerful noise around us came to a halt as everyone pulled out their phones in a panic. Some students screamed in excitement, while others looked devastated. The atmosphere instantly shifted from relaxation to tension.

My heart pounded in my chest. A wave of anxiety crashed over me as I hesitated to open the website. What if I hadn't passed? What if all my efforts had gone to waste? My hands trembled as I tapped on the result link, but at the last second, I closed my eyes and turned to Somya.

"I can't do this. You check for me," I whispered, my voice barely steady.

Somya took the phone, entered the details, and stared at the screen for a few seconds. Her eyes widened before a broad smile spread across her face.

"Aarna, you PASSED!" she shrieked, pulling me into a tight hug.

I let out a deep breath I hadn't realized I was holding. Relief flooded through me, and before I knew it, my friends were cheering and hugging me. Ayaan, standing a few feet away, locked eyes with me and gave me an approving nod with a small smile.

The moment was surreal. After months of dedication, sleepless nights, and self-doubt, I had done it. For the first time in a long while, I allowed myself to revel in the joy of my achievement.

Little did I know, this was just the beginning of what life had in store for me.

26

AYAAN

As I refreshed the results page for the third time, my heart raced. When the screen finally loaded, I could hardly believe my eyes: I had passed with distinction in Accounts, Law, and Economics. A surge of relief and pride washed over me.

Before I could fully process the news, I heard a familiar voice call out my name. Turning, I saw Aarna sprinting towards me, tears streaming down her face. For a split second, I feared something was wrong, but as she reached me, she threw her arms around me in a tight embrace.

"Ayaan, you did it! I'm so happy for you!" she exclaimed, her voice choked with emotion.

I hugged her back, feeling the warmth of her genuine happiness for me. "Thank you, Aarna. It means a lot."

Pulling back slightly, she looked up at me, her eyes glistening. "I knew you could do it."

In that moment, surrounded by the buzz of our classmates celebrating their own results, everything else faded away. Aarna's joy for my achievement made the months of hard work and sleepless nights worthwhile.

As we stood there, I couldn't help but think about how much she meant to me, and how this shared moment of success brought us even closer together.

27

AARNA

As the bus rumbled back towards the city, I couldn't contain my excitement. Clearing the CA exam on my first attempt was a monumental achievement, and sharing this success with my friends made it even sweeter. We had all worked tirelessly, and now, our efforts had paid off.

The atmosphere on the bus was electric. Laughter, cheers, and animated conversations filled the air as we celebrated our collective success. At one point, Kaira, Somya, Anu, and I exchanged gleeful glances, and without a word, we leaned into a spontaneous group hug. Our arms wrapped around each other tightly, a physical manifestation of our shared joy and relief. In that embrace, I felt an overwhelming sense of unity and accomplishment.

I was on cloud nine, basking in the joy of our achievements.

Suddenly, our sir stood up at the front of the bus, signaling for attention. The chatter gradually subsided as everyone turned to listen.

"Congratulations to all of you on passing your exams," he began, his voice steady and authoritative. "However, I must caution you against becoming overconfident. This is just the beginning. The next level will be even more challenging, and it will require greater dedication and hard work."

His words resonated deeply with me. The initial euphoria began to settle, replaced by a sober realization of the journey ahead. I knew he was right; this was a significant milestone, but it was not the end. The path to becoming a Chartered Accountant was long and demanding.

As the city lights flickered outside the bus window, I made a silent promise to myself. I would not let this success lead to complacency. I would channel this momentum into working even harder for the next level. The road ahead was daunting, but with determination and perseverance, I was ready to face the challenges that lay ahead.

28

AYAAN

Aarna had been eager to watch the latest blockbuster, and when she asked if I'd join her, I couldn't refuse. We decided to catch the evening show at our favorite cinema. The film was captivating, but I found myself equally engrossed in Aarna's reactions—the way her eyes lit up during exciting scenes and the soft laughter that escaped her during humorous moments.

After the movie, Aarna suggested we visit Cococart, a delightful chocolate store and café. We headed to the outlet at Parinee Crescenzo.

The aroma of rich cocoa greeted us as we entered, and the sight of beautifully arranged chocolates was a treat for the eyes.

Settling into a cozy corner, we ordered a selection of desserts and two steaming mugs of hot chocolate. The warmth of the drink was comforting, and the desserts were decadent, each bite melting in the mouth. We chatted about the movie, our future plans, and shared light-hearted stories, making the evening even more special.

As the night deepened, I offered to drop Aarna home. The drive was peaceful, the city lights casting a gentle glow on the streets. When we reached her place, she turned to me with a grateful smile.

"Thanks for tonight, Ayaan. I had a great time."

"Me too, Aarna. Let's do this again sometime."

She nodded, her eyes reflecting the promise of more shared moments. As she walked towards her door, I couldn't help but feel that this evening had brought us closer, deepening the bond we shared.

29

AARNA

The commencement of my CA Intermediate classes had ushered in a whirlwind of lectures, assignments, and relentless study sessions. The rigorous schedule left little room for leisure, making the prospect of a reunion with my school friends a beacon of excitement. When Simie floated the idea of gathering at Feelizza, a newly opened Italian restaurant in town, I eagerly embraced the opportunity to reconnect with Rishi, Jai, Saniya, Poorna, and Vihaan.

On the evening of our much-anticipated reunion, I stood before my mirror, contemplating my reflection. I had chosen a short black dress, its sleek fabric hugging my frame and revealing more skin than I was accustomed to. A surge of self-consciousness washed over me, but I quelled it with a determined smile. This was a night of celebration, a break from the monotony of studies, and I was resolved to enjoy it.

Feelizza exuded a warm and inviting ambiance. Soft, ambient lighting cast a golden hue over rustic wooden tables, and the air was infused with the tantalizing aroma of freshly baked bread and simmering marinara sauce. The gentle hum of chatter and clinking cutlery created a comforting symphony that set the perfect backdrop for our gathering.

As I approached our reserved table, I was greeted by the familiar faces of my friends, their expressions mirroring my own excitement. We exchanged hugs and pleasantries, the years melting away as we slipped back into the easy camaraderie of our school days. Noticing an empty seat beside me, I draped a napkin over my thighs, a feeble attempt to mask my earlier discomfort about my attire.

The evening unfolded with laughter and animated conversations. We reminisced about shared memories, each anecdote more hilarious than the last. The arrival of our pizzas—thin crusts adorned with vibrant toppings—was met with collective delight. The first bite was a revelation; the perfect harmony of tangy tomato sauce, creamy mozzarella, and fresh basil danced on my palate.

Amidst the merriment, Jai, in his characteristic exuberance, gesticulated wildly, inadvertently knocking over his glass. A cascade of water spilled across the table, the cool liquid seeping into my dress. A collective gasp ensued, followed by a flurry of napkins as everyone scrambled to contain the spill.

Before I could react, Rishi, who had arrived fashionably late and taken the seat beside me, leaned in close. His breath was warm against my ear as he whispered, "You don't need to feel uncomfortable, darling. It's me."

A shiver coursed through me, a mix of unease and something else I couldn't quite place. I forced a smile, my fingers tightening around the napkin on my lap. Glancing at Simie, I considered asking her to switch seats, but she was deep in conversation with Poorna, her laughter ringing out like a melody. Resigned, I nodded at Rishi, hoping to divert my attention back to the group.

Noticing the damp patches marring my dress, Rishi shrugged off his jacket and offered it to me. "Here, wrap this around your waist," he suggested, his tone gentle.

"Thank you," I murmured, accepting the jacket and tying it securely around me. The gesture was thoughtful, and I couldn't help but appreciate his chivalry, even as a lingering discomfort gnawed at me.

As the night deepened, we decided to capture the moment, snapping countless photos. Each click of the camera was a time capsule, preserving our laughter and the unspoken bond we shared. Reviewing the images, I was struck by a wave of nostalgia. The faces staring back at me were older, perhaps a bit wiser, but the essence of our friendship remained unchanged.

Leaving Feelizza, I felt a profound sense of contentment. The evening had been a delightful interlude, a reminder of the enduring connections that tethered us to our past. As I bid my friends goodnight, I couldn't help but look forward to our next reunion, whenever it might be.

30

AYAAN

Aarna's birthday was approaching, and I knew she had no intention of celebrating it. The memory of her previous birthday, where Rishi had abandoned her, still cast a shadow over her feelings about the day. But I couldn't bear the thought of her spending it alone, letting past hurts dictate her happiness. I decided to take matters into my own hands and plan a surprise to remind her of how cherished she truly is.

I reached out to Kaira, Somya, and Anu, her closest friends from college. We agreed to gather at her place just before midnight to usher in her birthday with warmth and love. Kaira suggested extending the invitation to Aarna's school friends as well, to make the celebration even more special. I hesitated, the image of Rishi's betrayal flashing in my mind.

"Let's keep it to her closest circle," I suggested gently. "We don't want any unexpected guests who might dampen her spirits."

Kaira understood immediately. "Got it. We'll make sure it's just the people who truly care about her."

As the clock inched closer to midnight, we gathered outside Aarna's apartment, each of us holding a small token of affection—a bouquet of her favorite lilies, a box of chocolates, and a handwritten note. The plan was simple: to surround her with love the moment her birthday began, to overwrite the painful memories with joyous ones.

At the stroke of twelve, we knocked on her door. Aarna opened it, her eyes widening in surprise as she took in the sight of us standing there, grinning like fools.

"Happy Birthday, Aarna!" we chorused, stepping inside to envelop her in a group hug.

Tears glistened in her eyes, but a genuine smile spread across her face. "You guys... I can't believe you did this."

"We couldn't let you spend your birthday alone," I said softly, handing her the lilies. "You deserve to be celebrated."

We spent the next few hours reminiscing, laughing, and simply enjoying each other's company. The room was filled with warmth and affection, a stark contrast to the loneliness she had felt the previous year.

As the night wore on, I caught Aarna's gaze. There was a lightness in her eyes that hadn't been there before, a silent acknowledgment that perhaps birthdays weren't so bad after all.

In that moment, I realized that this was all I ever wanted—to see her happy, to be the reason behind her smile. And as we sat there, surrounded by friends and love, I silently vowed to always be there for her, to ensure that she never had to face her fears alone again.

31

AARNA

The morning sun filtered through my curtains, casting a warm glow across my room. I stretched lazily, savoring the comfort of my bed, when a series of rapid knocks jolted me fully awake.

"Aarna! Open up!" Kaira's voice rang out, urgency lacing her tone.

I stumbled to the door, rubbing sleep from my eyes, and was greeted by the beaming faces of Kaira, Somya, Anu, and Ayaan. Their excitement was palpable, and I couldn't help but smile in return.

"Happy Birthday!" they chorused, thrusting a brightly wrapped package into my hands.

"What's this?" I asked, curiosity piqued.

"Open it and see!" Somya urged, practically bouncing on her toes.

Tearing into the wrapping, I uncovered a neatly organized folder. Flipping it open, I was met with flight tickets, hotel reservations, and a detailed itinerary. My heart skipped a beat as I read the destination: Goa.

"We're going to Goa?" I whispered, disbelief coloring my voice.

"Surprise!" Ayaan grinned. "Jai and Simie handled all the bookings. We're all set to leave this morning."

"But... I didn't pack anything." Panic began to bubble up.

"Already taken care of," Anu said, winking. "Your mom packed your bags. They're ready to go."

Overwhelmed, I felt tears prick at the corners of my eyes. "You all did this... for me?"

"Of course," Kaira said softly, pulling me into a hug. "You deserve the world, Aarna."

The next few hours were a whirlwind. We gathered at the airport, the group buzzing with excitement. Jai, Simie, Saniya, Vihaan, and the rest of my closest friends were all there, each contributing to this incredible surprise.

As we boarded the flight, I couldn't help but reflect on how blessed I was to have such thoughtful friends. The memory of last year's birthday, marred by disappointment, began to fade, replaced by the warmth of their love and effort.

The flight to Goa was filled with laughter and shared anticipation. Upon landing, the tropical breeze greeted us, carrying the scent of the sea and promise of adventure.

Our hotel was a charming boutique establishment nestled near the coastline. The rooms were cozy, adorned with local art, and offered stunning views of the ocean. After settling in, we convened in the lobby to discuss our plans.

"First stop, Palolem Beach," Jai announced, holding up the itinerary. "It's one of the most picturesque beaches here."

The day unfolded like a dream. We lounged on the golden sands of Palolem Beach, the sun kissing our skin as we dipped into the clear, azure waters. The beach was a crescent-shaped paradise, lined with swaying palm trees and vibrant shacks offering refreshing coconut water and delectable Goan snacks.

As the sun began its descent, painting the sky in hues of orange and pink, we made our way to a quaint beachside café. Fairy lights twinkled overhead, and the sound of gentle waves provided the perfect backdrop to our evening.

"To Aarna," Ayaan toasted, raising his glass. "May this birthday mark the beginning of countless adventures and cherished memories."

I smiled, clinking my glass with theirs. "Thank you all. This means more to me than words can express."

The night was filled with laughter, stories, and the deepening of bonds. As I looked around at the faces of my dearest friends, I realized that this trip was more than just a birthday celebration; it was a testament to the love and friendship that enriched my life.

The morning sun streamed through the curtains of our cozy Goan villa, casting a warm glow that promised another day of adventure. The previous day had been a whirlwind of excitement, and as I stretched lazily, I couldn't help but smile at the thought of what lay ahead.

After a leisurely breakfast of fresh fruit and Goan poi bread, the group decided to explore the vibrant Anjuna Flea Market. The market was a sensory overload, with stalls displaying colorful textiles, handcrafted jewelry, and aromatic spices. Laughter echoed as we haggled with vendors and tried on quirky accessories.

As the sun dipped below the horizon, painting the sky in hues of orange and pink, we returned to our villa to prepare for the evening. Jai and Simie had planned a beachside party at a secluded spot they had discovered earlier—a perfect blend of tranquility and celebration.

The beach house was adorned with twinkling fairy lights, and a bonfire crackled softly, adding to the ambiance. Music played in the background as we danced barefoot in the sand, the cool breeze carrying the scent of the ocean.

Feeling adventurous, I decided to indulge in a few more drinks than usual. The world around me became a delightful blur, and my inhibitions melted away. At some point, I stumbled, and strong arms caught me before I hit the ground.

"Easy there, Aarna," Rishi's voice murmured close to my ear.

I looked up to see his concerned eyes studying me. "Thanks, Rishi."

"Maybe it's time to take a break," he suggested gently.

He led me away from the crowd to a quieter spot on the beach. We sat down, the cool sand beneath us, and the rhythmic sound of waves providing a soothing backdrop.

"You didn't have to, you know," I said, feeling a mix of gratitude and embarrassment.

"I wanted to," he replied simply.

We sat in comfortable silence for a while, the moon casting a silvery glow on the water. The alcohol had dulled my usual reservations, and I found myself leaning closer to him.

"Dance with me," I whispered impulsively.

He looked surprised but stood up, extending his hand. We swayed gently to the distant music, the world narrowing down to just the two of us.

Without thinking, I closed the gap between us, pressing my lips to his. The kiss was soft, tentative, and filled with unspoken emotions.

When we finally pulled apart, I saw a flicker of something in his eyes—confusion, perhaps, or maybe longing.

"Aarna, I..." he began, but the words were lost as we heard someone approaching.

Turning, I saw Ayaan standing a few feet away, his expression unreadable.

"Everything okay here?" he asked, his voice tight.

"Yeah, just needed some air," I replied, trying to sound casual.

Ayaan's eyes flicked between Rishi and me, and I could sense the tension building.

"We should head back," Ayaan said, his tone leaving little room for argument.

As we walked back to the group, I couldn't shake the feeling that the dynamics between us had shifted, and I wondered what the rest of the trip would hold.

32

RISHI

The night air was thick with the scent of salt and the distant hum of waves crashing against the shore. As I lay in bed, the events of the evening replayed incessantly in my mind, each detail more vivid than the last.

Aarna had always been beautiful, but tonight, in that red V-necked gown that hugged her every curve, she was mesmerizing. The way the fabric clung to her, the way it accentuated her silhouette—it was as if she had stepped out of a dream. I couldn't take my eyes off her, and it seemed neither could anyone else.

But it wasn't just her appearance that captivated me; it was the way she moved, the way she laughed, the way her eyes sparkled under the moonlight. Every gesture, every glance, drew me in deeper, ensnaring me in a web of emotions I hadn't anticipated.

And then, the kiss.

It had taken me by surprise. One moment, we were dancing, lost in the rhythm of the night, and the next, her lips were on mine. Soft, warm, and tasting faintly of the wine she'd been sipping earlier. For a heartbeat, I was too stunned to react, but then instinct took over. I pulled her closer, deepening the kiss, losing myself in the sensation.

Was it the alcohol that had prompted her to kiss me? Perhaps. But in that moment, it felt real. The world around us faded away, leaving just the two of us, connected in a way we had never been before.

As I lay there, staring at the ceiling, I couldn't help but wonder what this meant. Was it a fleeting moment, born out of the night's festivities, or was it the beginning of something more? The uncertainty gnawed at me, a mix of hope and fear swirling in my chest.

I turned over, trying to find a comfortable position, but sleep eluded me. Every time I closed my eyes, I saw her face, felt the press of her lips against mine, heard the soft gasp she made as our kiss deepened.

Damn it, Rishi, get a grip, I chastised myself. But it was no use. I was in too deep, and there was no turning back now.

With a resigned sigh, I sat up and swung my legs over the side of the bed. Maybe a walk would clear my head. I grabbed a shirt and headed out, the cool night air a welcome contrast to the turmoil inside me.

As I wandered along the shoreline, the events of the night replayed over and over, each iteration leaving me more confused than the last. But amidst the confusion, one thing was clear: I couldn't stop thinking about Aarna, and that kiss had changed everything.

The question now was, what was I going to do about it?

33

AARNA

The sun hung high in the Goan sky, casting shimmering reflections on the azure waters as we gathered for a day of water sports. The excitement was palpable, with everyone eager to indulge in the adventures that awaited. Jet skiing, parasailing, and banana boat rides were on the agenda, promising a day filled with thrills.

As the instructors began pairing us up for the speedboat rides, I noticed that, by coincidence, it was just Rishi, Ayaan, and me left without partners. A fleeting tension passed between us, but we quickly masked it with smiles.

"Looks like it's the three of us," Ayaan remarked, trying to lighten the mood.

We boarded the speedboat, the engine roaring to life as we sped across the waves. The wind whipped through my hair, and for a moment, I felt a liberating sense of freedom. But beneath the surface, emotions churned.

As the boat took a sharp turn, I lost my balance and tumbled forward, landing against Rishi. My hand pressed against his bare abs , the warmth of his skin sending an unexpected jolt through me. Our eyes met, and for a heartbeat, the world seemed to pause.

"Are you okay?" Rishi's voice was soft, filled with concern.

Before I could respond, Ayaan reached out, helping me back to my seat. "Careful there," he said, positioning himself between Rishi and me.

The remainder of the ride was a blur. Ayaan attempted to engage us in conversation, alternating between reminiscing about college days with Rishi and asking me about my birthday. But my mind was elsewhere, replaying the brief contact with Rishi and the unspoken tension that lingered.

As we disembarked, I couldn't shake the feeling that the dynamics between the three of us had shifted, leaving me with more questions than answers.

34

RISHI

The moment Aarna stepped onto the sun-kissed sands of Palolem Beach, I forgot how to breathe. My world reduced to just her, bathed in golden light, the sound of crashing waves a mere background to the way she took my breath away.

She wore a white bikini that hugged her curves like a dream, the contrast against her sun-bronzed skin making her look like some ethereal goddess. The top had delicate lace trimmings, subtle yet elegant, with thin straps that tied behind her neck, accentuating the graceful slope of her shoulders. The matching bottoms sat low on her waist, with strings tied at her hips, playful bows swaying slightly with the ocean breeze. It wasn't just the swimsuit, though—it was the way she wore it. Effortlessly. Like she belonged here, under this sun, in the midst of a thousand admiring stares, yet untouched by any of them.

Her long, wavy hair cascaded over her back, the ends damp from an earlier dip in the sea. Aarna had always been beautiful, but today... today she was something else. A vision. The kind you only read about in poetry but never quite believe to be real. Her accessories were simple but well-chosen—a dainty seashell anklet that jingled softly with her every step, a thin gold chain around her neck catching the sunlight, and round-framed sunglasses perched atop her head. She exuded an effortless kind of elegance, the kind that didn't require effort at all. It was just... her.

I stood frozen for a long moment, fingers clenched into fists, trying to maintain some semblance of self-control. But damn, it was impossible. Every part of me just wanted to close the distance between us, wrap my arms around her, and bury my face into the crook of her neck. Just hold her. Keep her there, right where I could feel her heartbeat against mine.

She walked towards me, barefoot, her toes sinking into the warm sand, her lips curving into the smallest of smirks. She knew. She knew exactly what she was doing to me. The teasing glint in her eyes confirmed it.

"You're staring," she said, her voice laced with amusement.

"Am I?" I asked, voice rougher than I intended. "Not my fault you decided to show up looking like that."

She let out a soft laugh, tilting her head, and damn, even that simple action made my heart clench. "Like what?"

"Like you're trying to ruin me."

Aarna bit her lower lip, her cheeks turning the faintest shade of pink. The sight of it nearly undid me. My fingers itched to trace along her jaw, to pull her in, to erase the space between us.

But before I could act on any of it, she turned on her heel and walked towards the water, casting a glance over her shoulder. "Come on, Rishi. Race you to the waves?"

I swallowed hard, exhaling a shaky breath before running a hand through my hair. If this was what Goa had

in store for me, I was in serious trouble.
And I wasn't sure I minded one bit.

35

AYAAN

The sun had dipped below the horizon, casting a warm glow over the Goan resort as we gathered to celebrate Aarna's birthday. The air was thick with anticipation, but beneath my practiced smile, a storm brewed. Every shared glance, every whispered word between Rishi and Aarna felt like a dagger twisting deeper into my chest.

I tried to focus on the festivities, to lose myself in the laughter and chatter of our friends, but my eyes betrayed me, constantly drifting back to them. The ease with which they interacted, the unspoken understanding that seemed to flow between them—it was unbearable.

Just as I was about to excuse myself, the door to Aarna's room creaked open. Time seemed to slow as she stepped out, and the world around me faded into a blur.

She wore a black bodycon dress that clung to her figure, accentuating every curve. Strategic cutouts at her waist offered tantalizing glimpses of her skin, and the neckline dipped just enough to hint at her cleavage without being overt. Her hair cascaded over her shoulders in loose waves, and a simple pendant rested just above the neckline, drawing the eye.

In that moment, all my jealousy, all my resentment melted away, replaced by sheer admiration. She was breathtaking.

As she approached, the room seemed to hold its breath. Her eyes met mine, and she offered a shy smile, a faint blush coloring her cheeks.

"Happy birthday, Aarna," I managed to say, my voice betraying none of the turmoil within.

"Thank you, Ayaan," she replied softly.

The evening progressed in a haze of toasts, laughter, and shared memories. But as the time came to cut the cake, a palpable tension settled over the group. Tradition dictated that the birthday person would offer the first bite to someone special.

Aarna stood before the cake, knife in hand, her gaze flickering between Rishi and me. The seconds stretched into eternity as I held my breath, waiting.

Finally, she sliced a piece, lifting it delicately. Her eyes met mine once more, and for a fleeting moment, I dared to hope.

But then, with a graceful turn, she extended the bite to Rishi.

A polite cheer rose from the group, but I barely heard it over the roaring in my ears. I forced a smile, clapping along, but inside, I was crumbling.

The rest of the night passed in a blur. I laughed in all the right places, joined in the celebrations, but my heart wasn't in it. All I could think about was the look in Aarna's eyes as she fed Rishi that first bite, a look that spoke of a connection I could never hope to share.

As the party wound down and guests began to drift away, I found myself alone on the balcony, staring out at the moonlit sea. The sound of footsteps approached, and I turned to see Aarna standing there, concern etched on her face.

"Ayaan, are you okay?" she asked gently.

"Yeah, just needed some fresh air," I replied, forcing a smile.

She stepped closer, placing a hand on my arm. "Thank you for being here. It means a lot to me."

I looked into her eyes, searching for any hint of deeper affection, but all I saw was friendship. Nodding, I patted her hand. "Always, Aarna."

As she walked away, I turned back to the sea, the weight of unspoken feelings pressing heavily on my chest. In the distance, the waves crashed against the shore, a melancholic symphony to mirror the turmoil within.

36

AARNA

The golden sun had long set, but the night carried with it a soft warmth, the air laced with the scent of the ocean. The celebration had been in full swing, laughter echoing around, but something felt off.

I sat there, the remnants of my birthday cake in front of me, when I noticed Ayaan. He was leaning against the wooden railing, his white shirt crisp against his tanned skin, the top button undone in a way that made him look effortlessly good. His beige pants fit snugly, emphasizing his lean build. But it wasn't his looks that held my attention—it was his expression.

Ayaan wasn't laughing. He wasn't even smiling. His jaw was set, his arms crossed as he gazed out into the night, detached from the energy around him.

And then it hit me.

The first bite. I had given the first bite of my birthday cake to Rishi.

A lump formed in my throat as I grabbed a small bowl, scooping out a generous portion of cake. I knew Ayaan well enough to recognize when something was bothering him, and this? This was definitely about that moment.

Taking a deep breath, I walked over, my heart picking up pace. "Ayaan?"

He turned slightly, his sharp eyes meeting mine, unreadable. Up close, I could see the flicker of hurt hidden beneath his otherwise composed expression.

"What's wrong?" I asked softly, extending the bowl to him.

He exhaled slowly before shaking his head. "Nothing, Aarna. Enjoy your night."

I frowned. "Ayaan, don't do that. Don't pretend you're fine when you're clearly not."

He hesitated for a moment before finally speaking. "It's nothing, really. Just—" His gaze locked onto mine, searching, questioning. "You and Rishi are just friends, right?"

I blinked, surprised by his question. "Of course. That's all we've ever been."

He let out a hollow chuckle, shaking his head. "Then why did you kiss him that day at the beach?"

The words struck me like lightning. My breath hitched, my mind scrambling for an answer. But there was none.

Because I didn't know why.

I had acted on impulse, on emotion, on something I couldn't even begin to explain. But that didn't change the fact that it had happened.

Ayaan's gaze was unwavering, waiting. But I had nothing to say.

So I did the only thing I could—I turned and walked away, the weight of his question settling deep in my chest.

37

AYAAN

Thalassa was buzzing with energy when we arrived, the sea breeze carrying the faint scent of salt and liquor. Music pulsed through the open-air venue, a mix of deep bass and sultry melodies that vibrated in my chest. The place was alive with laughter, the clinking of glasses, and the carefree energy that only a Goan night could offer. But none of it compared to her.

Aarna stepped in like she owned the night, and for a moment, I forgot to breathe. She wore a black net top that clung to her, teasing just enough to drive anyone crazy, paired with high-waisted black denim shorts that hugged her hips and accentuated the long, golden glow of her legs. The pearls in her hair shimmered under the lights, contrasting against the dark waves that cascaded down her back. Her makeup was soft—subtle kohl lining her eyes—but it was her lips that stole the show. A dark shade, bold and unshaken, making a statement without her even trying. She had always been beautiful, but tonight, she was something else entirely. Untouchable. Dangerous.

My jaw clenched as I noticed the way people were looking at her. Men, their eyes lingering too long, appreciating too much. My fingers twitched, but I forced myself to stay still. I had no claim over her. No right to step in. So I just watched, every muscle in my body tight as she moved, laughing, swaying to the music.

We found our spot near the bar, ordering drinks as the night unfolded. The laughter, the teasing—it was all easy, but my attention never wavered from her. She was the center of it all, pulling people into her orbit like she was made of gravity. Rishi stood beside her, their chemistry undeniable, the way they leaned into each other, the way he knew just what to say to make her throw her head back in laughter. And all I could do was sit back and drown in it, sip after sip, drink after drink.

Then she did something that made my heart stop.

With a mischievous glint in her eye, she climbed onto the bar table, her fingers trailing against the wooden surface as she steadied herself. The music shifted—louder, wilder—and Aarna threw her hands into the air, letting the beat take over. The crowd erupted, cheering her on as she swayed her hips, her body moving in perfect rhythm. Confidence radiated from her, and she reveled in it, completely lost in the moment.

I couldn't look away.

But neither could anyone else.

I saw them—strangers, their gazes dark with interest, their whispers barely concealed. Every second that passed made my grip on the glass tighter, my blood hotter. I wanted to pull her down, wrap my jacket around her, tell her that she didn't need an audience to know she was electric. But I stayed rooted in place, my lips pressed into a firm line. She wasn't mine to protect. She never had been.

Jai leaned in, nudging me. "She's a firecracker tonight."

I gave a short nod, unable to find words. Because how was I supposed to explain the storm inside me? How could I put into words the battle between wanting to let her be free and wanting to keep her to myself?

Minutes blurred into an hour, and soon, the drinks caught up to her. Aarna wobbled, a lazy grin on her lips as she giggled at something no one else had heard. Rishi was at her side in an instant, steadying her before she could fall. Jai followed right after, throwing an arm around her shoulders. She was completely drunk, her laughter slurred, her head resting against Rishi's shoulder as she mumbled something incoherent.

"We need to get her back," Rishi said, his voice steady despite the alcohol coursing through him.

Jai nodded, already leading the way through the crowded venue. I followed behind them, watching as Rishi held her close, whispering something into her ear that made her smile sleepily. It should've been me. I hated that it wasn't.

By the time we reached the villa, it was 4 a.m., the night sky fading into hints of dawn. Rishi helped Aarna to her room, and I stood by the door, feeling like an outsider. Watching. Wanting. But knowing I could do nothing about it.

I turned away before I could hate myself more.

38

AARNA

I groaned as I turned over in bed, my head pounding like a drum. The sunlight filtering through the curtains felt like an interrogation light, and I pulled the blanket over my face, trying to piece together the night before. My throat was parched, my limbs ached, and an unsettling mix of exhaustion and exhilaration pulsed through me.

"You're finally up?" Simie's amused voice rang through the room.

I peeked out from the blanket and squinted at Simie, who was sitting cross-legged on the bed next to mine. Anu and a couple of the other girls were lounging on the couch, watching me with expectant smirks.

"Why are you all looking at me like that? What happened?" My voice was raspy, and I reached for the glass of water on my bedside table.

Anu chuckled. "Oh, you mean you don't remember?"

Simie rolled her eyes dramatically. "Aarna, babe, you were the star of the show last night."

I blinked. "What do you mean? What did I do?"

The girls exchanged knowing glances before bursting into laughter.

"You climbed onto the bar table at Thalassa and danced like nobody was watching," Anu finally spilled, grinning.

I gasped. "No way!"

Simie nodded. "Oh, yes way. You were completely in your element. Flipping your hair, waving your arms, and that outfit? Girl, you looked fire."

I felt a rush of warmth spread across my cheeks. "I actually did that? I've never done anything like that before."

"And you were absolutely killing it," Somya piped in. "People were cheering, some even took videos."

I groaned, burying my face in my hands. "Videos? Oh god, please tell me I didn't do anything embarrassing."

Anu shrugged. "Depends on what you call embarrassing. You were bold, confident, and having the time of your life. And then, of course, there was Ayaan."

My head snapped up. "Ayaan? What about him?"

Simie smirked. "Oh, nothing much. Just that he couldn't take his eyes off you. He looked ready to murder any guy who even thought about coming close to you."

A rush of memories started to surface—fragments of music, laughter, Rishi and Jai helping me out of the club. I groaned again. "Tell me I didn't make a fool of myself in front of him."

Anu smirked. "Depends on how you see it. He was definitely watching you all night. But honestly, Aarna, you should be proud. You had fun, you let go, and you lived in the moment. That's something to celebrate."

A slow smile crept onto my lips as I processed their words. Maybe they were right. Maybe, for once, I had truly lived without overthinking every little thing. And oddly enough, I was kind of proud of myself for it.

39

AYAAN

The morning air was thick with the bittersweet feeling of departure. In just a few hours, we would be boarding our flight back to Mumbai, and the trip that had been nothing short of chaotic, breathtaking, and utterly unforgettable would come to an end. But before that happened, I wanted to do something—one last thing. Something that had been on my mind since we arrived in Goa.

I wanted to take Aarna to the church my mother had once taken me to when I was just five years old.

It wasn't the grandest church, not the one tourists crowded for photos, but it held meaning. It stood on a quiet hill, slightly away from the city noise, its white walls standing tall against the sky. As a kid, I remembered staring at the stained-glass windows, mesmerized by how the sunlight painted the marble floors in a kaleidoscope of colors. Back then, I hadn't understood much about faith or prayers, but I had felt something in that space—peace, maybe.

I had no idea why I wanted Aarna to come with me, only that I did.

When I asked her, half-expecting her to decline, she surprised me. She didn't hesitate, didn't throw a sarcastic remark or ask why. She simply nodded. "Okay, let's go."

An hour later, she stepped out of her room in a simple white dress, the fabric flowing lightly around her as the wind toyed with the strands of her hair. She looked different from the girl who had danced on the bar last night, from the girl who made heads turn at every party. This version of Aarna—soft, effortless, unguarded—was something else entirely.

The drive there was silent, comfortable in a way I wasn't used to. When we reached the church, I watched her take it in. The structure was old, standing proud despite the cracks that had started to show with time. The wooden doors creaked as we stepped inside, and the faint scent of wax and old books filled the air.

She didn't say anything as we walked towards the pews. Sunlight streamed through the stained-glass windows, painting her skin in hues of blue, red, and gold. I glanced at her, half-wondering what she was thinking, but she simply stared ahead, as if she, too, felt the same inexplicable sense of calm I had all those years ago.

"It's beautiful," she murmured after a while, her voice quiet, reverent.

I nodded, watching as she traced a finger along the wooden bench, her expression unreadable. "I haven't been here in years."

"Why today?" she asked, turning to me. "Why did you want to come back?"

I hesitated. "I don't know. I guess... I wanted to remember something from before everything got complicated. Before life became about choices and consequences and people we can't have."

Her gaze flickered with something I couldn't name, something that made my pulse unsteady. She didn't push, didn't ask for more. Instead, she exhaled and leaned back slightly, looking up at the ceiling adorned with faded paintings of angels and saints.

"Maybe that's why places like this exist," she said after a beat. "So we can forget for a little while. Or remember what we need to."

I didn't reply, because somehow, she had already said everything I was feeling.

We sat there in silence, letting the weight of the past few days settle around us. For once, there were no interruptions, no knowing glances from Rishi, no teasing remarks from the others. Just us, in this quiet space where the world didn't demand anything from us.

And for that moment, it was enough.

40

AARNA

The moment I stepped out of the airport, Mumbai greeted me with its familiar chaos. The honking of impatient taxi drivers, the distant roar of a train passing by, and the chatter of people haggling with street vendors filled the air. The humidity clung to my skin, a stark contrast to the cool Goan breeze I had grown used to over the past few days. The city was alive, restless, and somehow, despite living here all my life, it felt overwhelming after the peaceful escape I had just returned from.

As we drove home, I stared out of the window, watching the blur of neon lights and billboards, each one screaming for attention. The roads were packed with cars that barely moved, and the aroma of roadside food stalls mixed with the sharp scent of petrol. I let out a deep breath, feeling an emptiness settle inside me. The trip was over, and I wasn't ready to return to reality just yet.

Once home, I dragged my suitcase into my room and collapsed on my bed, feeling the weight of exhaustion press against my body. But sleep didn't come easy. My mind was still stuck in Goa, reliving every moment, every laugh, every careless night spent under the stars. It felt unreal how quickly it had all ended.

With a sigh, I grabbed my phone and scrolled through the pictures from the trip. There we were, grinning at the beach, posing in front of the villa, dancing wildly at Thalassa. Each image was a frozen memory, proof that it had all been real. My finger hovered over one particular picture—the church. The soft sunlight filtering through the stained-glass windows, the quiet serenity of the place. And beside me, Ayaan.

I swallowed hard. Ayaan.

A strange pang of guilt settled in my chest. I wasn't sure why. Maybe because he had been so genuine, so open, and I had just taken everything at face value without thinking about how he felt. Maybe because I had let myself get caught up in moments without considering the consequences. Or maybe because, deep down, I knew he deserved more than the half-hearted emotions I could offer.

I shook my head, pushing the thoughts away. I had promised myself something in Goa. For once, I would choose myself. Not Rishi, not Ayaan, not anyone else. Just me.

I wasn't going to apologize for wanting to be selfish. Not this time.

Just then, my phone buzzed with a message from Simie. Back to the madness, huh? I smiled faintly and typed back, Yep. Feels weird.

A few seconds later, she replied, We should meet soon. I miss everyone already.

I exhaled and set my phone down. Maybe meeting them would help. Maybe it would make the transition back to normal life easier. But as I lay there, staring at the ceiling, I knew one thing for sure—Goa had changed something in me. And I wasn't sure if I would ever be the same again.

ꔸꔸꔸ

I walked into Café Kala Ghoda, the comforting scent of roasted coffee beans and freshly baked croissants wrapping around me like a warm hug. The place was buzzing with the usual crowd—artists lost in their sketchbooks, freelancers typing away, and couples sharing whispered conversations. But my eyes scanned past all of them, searching for Jai.

There he was, seated by the large French window, drumming his fingers against the rim of his coffee cup. His ever-present smirk widened as he spotted me approaching. "Look who finally decided to grace me with her presence," he teased, standing up to pull me into a quick hug.

I rolled my eyes and plopped down across from him. "Shut up. I needed this coffee more than you can imagine."

Jai chuckled, flagging down a waiter to order me my usual caramel latte. "Alright, spill. What's going on inside that chaotic little head of yours?"

I let out a dramatic sigh, swirling my spoon through the sugar bowl absentmindedly. "I kissed Rishi."

Jai nearly choked on his coffee, coughing as he grabbed a napkin. "Wait. Back up. What?"

"Yeah." I groaned, burying my face in my hands. "It happened in Goa. And now, I have no idea what to do. I mean... we've had feelings for each other for so long, but then there's Ayaan."

Jai raised an eyebrow, setting his cup down. "Ayaan?"

I hesitated, staring at the table. "He's just... really hot, Jai. And I don't know if it's just the thrill or something deeper, but I feel something. And it's messing with my head."

Jai snorted. "You're telling me you're torn between two ridiculously good-looking guys who are crazy about you? Wow, Aarna, such a tough life."

I threw a sugar packet at him. "I'm serious!"

He held up his hands in surrender, laughing. "Okay, okay. Look, I know you. You don't get confused like this unless it's real. So, maybe instead of trying to pick a side, you take a step back and figure out what you want. Not what Rishi wants, not what Ayaan wants. Just you."

I stared at him, his words settling deep within me. "That... actually makes sense."

"Of course, it does." He winked. "I'm the wise one, remember?"

I rolled my eyes but felt lighter. Jai always had a way of making things seem less complicated. The rest of our time at the café was spent laughing over old memories, stealing bites of each other's desserts, and making fun of the pretentious guy reading poetry two tables away.

By the time we left, the sun had started its descent, casting a golden glow over the streets of Mumbai. Jai pulled up his car outside the café, and I climbed in, rolling the windows down.

"Time for some therapy," he declared, grinning as he scrolled through his playlist.

The first notes of our favorite song filled the car, and without hesitation, we both started singing at the top of our lungs. The streets blurred past us, the wind whipping through my hair, but in that moment, I felt free. No Rishi, no Ayaan, no confusion. Just me and Jai, screaming lyrics and laughing like we had no worries in the world.

As he pulled up outside my building, he turned to me. "You'll figure it out, Aarna. You always do."

I smiled, squeezing his hand. "Thanks for today."

"Anytime," he said, winking. "Now, get inside before your mom starts thinking I've kidnapped you."

I laughed, stepping out and waving as he drove off. As I made my way upstairs, I realized something—maybe Jai was right. Maybe, for once, I needed to stop overthinking and just let life happen.

41

AYAAN

The weight of the upcoming CA Intermediate exams was beginning to settle over all of us like a thick cloud. The trip to Goa felt like a fever dream now, something distant and untouched by the reality of financial management, corporate laws, and tax regulations looming over our heads. Three months. That's all we had, and the backlog wasn't kind.

I had spent the past week buried under balance sheets and case laws, trying to make sense of the mountain of topics I had yet to master. The guilt of wasted time clawed at me, but there was no point dwelling on it. The only way out was through.

Aarna was coming over today. She wanted to go over receivables management in financial management, and I had a few doubts regarding dividends in business law. It was the perfect exchange. I was always better with numbers, and she had an iron grip on legal concepts. It made sense to study together. But if I was being honest, I just wanted to see her again.

I glanced at the clock. She'd be here soon. The least I could do was make her favorite pasta before we buried ourselves in books. Cooking had always been my escape, my way of controlling something when everything else felt chaotic. I tossed the pasta into boiling water, chopping up fresh basil for the sauce. By the time she rang the doorbell, the apartment was filled with the rich aroma of tomatoes andbutter.

Aarna stepped in, her hair in a loose bun, dressed in an oversized sweatshirt and leggings. She looked like she had barely slept, her dark circles betraying the pressure we were all under.

"You look like you just wrestled with taxation laws," I teased, stepping aside to let her in.

"I did," she groaned, dropping her books on the table. "And lost."

"Well, I made your favorite pasta, so consider it a consolation prize."

Her eyes lit up for a moment before she quickly masked it with an exaggerated smirk. "Impressive, Sharma. Are you trying to bribe me into tutoring you?"

"Is it working?"

She picked up a fork and took a bite, closing her eyes for a second. "Maybe."

We settled down at the dining table, books and notes spread between us as we ate. The study session started off slow, both of us flipping through pages, trying to get into the zone. But eventually, we found our rhythm. I explained cash conversion cycles and collection policies, and she walked me through the finer details of interim and final dividends.

Somewhere in the middle of it, she started doodling on the edge of my notebook, tiny stars and flowers in ink. I watched her for a second, the way her fingers absentmindedly twirled her pen, the way she tilted her head when she was explaining something complex. She looked at home, sitting across from me like this, like we had done this a hundred times before.

Four hours passed in a blur. When we finally leaned back, stretching our stiff muscles, I felt something I hadn't in weeks—contentment.

"This was productive," Aarna admitted, rubbing her temples. "I might actually not fail FM now."

I chuckled. "Well, at least one of us is surviving this exam."

She smirked, gathering her books. "Oh, you're surviving too. You have me."

I watched her as she packed up, her words hanging in the air between us. There were so many ways to interpret them, but I chose the simplest one. For now, I had her. Even if it was just over balance sheets and dividend policies, I had her.

And that was enough.

42

AARNA

Studying with Ayaan had become second nature to me. What started as a simple session to go over Receivables Management had now extended into something much bigger. Every day, we tackled a new subject—Tax, Audit, Strategic Management—diving deep into the endless syllabus that awaited us.

It was strange how comfortable it felt. There was no pressure, no expectations—just two people trying to survive the nightmare that was CA Intermediate. And somehow, amidst all the stress, Ayaan made it feel lighter. Whenever I'd groan about formulas or complain about having to read another audit standard, he'd just chuckle, shake his head, and push a plate of food toward me.

He always made sure we were eating well. "Brain food," he called it. But I knew better—it was just his way of taking care of me. And I didn't mind it one bit.

Mock exams were now just around the corner, and the weight of it was starting to get to me. No matter how much I studied, there was always something I hadn't covered, something that made me doubt myself. The anxiety had started creeping in, making my stomach churn every time I looked at my planner.

"You're doing great," Ayaan told me one evening when I had my head buried in my hands. "You just need to trust yourself a little more."

It was easier said than done, but hearing it from him made it slightly more believable.

Still, I needed a break.

So, I called up Anu and Simie and asked if they were free. Anu, as expected, was buried under her own mountain of books, but she agreed to meet me for an hour. Simie, who had just wrapped up her internship, was more than happy to join.

We met at Marine Drive, our favorite spot in the city. The moment I saw them, I felt like I could breathe again. The air was cool, the waves crashing against the rocks, and the city lights reflecting off the water. For the first time in weeks, I let myself relax.

"So, what's new?" Simie asked, stretching her legs out in front of her.

I hesitated for a moment before finally admitting, "Ayaan and I have been studying together a lot."

Anu's eyebrows shot up. "A lot, huh?" she smirked. "And how's that going?"

I rolled my eyes at her tone, but the blush creeping up my neck betrayed me. "It's just studying."

"Uh-huh. Studying. That's all?" Anu teased, nudging me playfully.

Simie, ever the practical one, just sighed. "Look, whatever's going on, just make sure you're focusing on your exams. You'll regret it later if you don't."

I nodded, knowing she was right. But that didn't stop the warmth from spreading through me when I thought about Ayaan. How his presence made things feel easier. How, even in the worst moments of panic, he had a way of grounding me.

I wasn't sure what it meant. And I wasn't ready to think about it yet.

For now, I just needed to pass these damn exams.

43

AYAAN

I stretched my arms above my head, groaning as I flipped through the last few pages of the consolidation chapter. My brain felt fried, but at least we were almost done. Aarna sat across from me, aggressively highlighting sections in her notebook like her life depended on it.

"Aarna, I swear if you highlight one more line, the book is going to protest," I said, rubbing my eyes.

She glared at me but didn't stop. "Let me be, Ayaan. If I don't highlight, how will I find the important stuff later?"

I smirked. "Everything is important if you highlight the entire page."

She rolled her eyes and flipped the page.

We had been studying for hours now, tackling Advanced Accounting like warriors in battle. Amalgamation had drained the life out of us, but consolidation was the final boss. And then there was the dreaded AS 20 – Earnings Per Share.

I closed my book dramatically. "You know, AS 20 is basically just a breakup lesson. If you divide too much, your value just keeps decreasing."

Aarna blinked at me, then burst out laughing, clutching her stomach. "Ayaan, what the hell?!"

"I'm serious!" I grinned. "Diluted EPS is what happens when you move on too fast."

She laughed so hard that she almost fell off the chair. "Stop it! I won't be able to unsee this during the exam!"

"Exactly my plan," I smirked, leaning back. "Now, whenever you see AS 20, you'll remember me."

Aarna threw a pen at me, still laughing. "Idiot."

"Genius," I corrected.

We finally finished consolidation, and I could see the exhaustion setting in for both of us. Aarna was staring at the table like she was calculating all her life decisions.

"What's up?" I asked, even though I knew.

She sighed, tapping her pen against the notebook. "The accounts mock tomorrow. I feel like I know nothing. What if I blank out?"

I shook my head. "You won't. We just revised everything. Trust yourself."

"Easy for you to say. You don't have an internal panic mode activated at all times," she muttered.

I grinned. "No, but I do have a foolproof plan."

She raised an eyebrow. "Which is?"

"We finish studying, you get a full night's sleep, and tomorrow, you walk into that exam hall like the Accounts Queen you are."

Aarna snorted. "Accounts Queen?"

"Do you want confidence or do you want accuracy?" I smirked.

She sighed, shaking her head with a small smile. "Fine. I'll try to believe in myself."

"Good," I said. "Because after all this, if you don't top the mocks, I'm demanding a refund on all my tutoring services."

She playfully smacked my arm. "No refunds."

I grinned. "Exactly. So go kill that mock test tomorrow."

AARNA

The weight of exhaustion settled heavily on my shoulders as I finally put my pen down. My first set of mocks was over, and while Group 1 had gone somewhat okay, Group 2 had been an absolute disaster. Audit, in particular, felt like a cruel joke, a series of questions I barely managed to grasp. I exhaled sharply, rubbing my temples as I stared at my desk, a half-empty cup of coffee growing cold beside me.

Ayaan had called me an hour after our last paper, sounding equally worn out. "How was it?" he asked, his voice lacking its usual cocky confidence.

"Terrible," I admitted. "I don't think I'm passing at this rate."

He let out a tired chuckle. "Join the club. I don't even want to think about Audit. I swear the paper was set by someone who wanted us all to fail."

"Exactly!" I groaned, leaning back against my chair. "And don't even get me started on SM. I blanked out on that one long answer."

"Same," he muttered. "But you know what? It's just mocks. The real thing is what matters."

"Yeah, but what if I mess up the real thing too?" I asked, my anxiety creeping in. "I've been working so hard, Ayaan. What if it's not enough?"

He was silent for a second before speaking, his voice firm. "It will be. I've seen you. You're literally the most disciplined person I know when it comes to studying. Stop doubting yourself."

I sighed, a small smile tugging at my lips. "You're a good friend, you know that?"

"I'm aware," he teased. "Now go rest. You deserve at least one night off before we bury ourselves in books again."

After hanging up, I texted Anu, still feeling overwhelmed. Me: "What if I actually fail? This is a real possibility. My audit paper was a nightmare."

Anu: "Aarna, shut up. You are not failing."

Me: "No, but seriously, it was so bad."

Anu: "Okay, maybe it was bad. But you know what? Everyone found it bad. You're not alone. And also, please tell me why Ayaan is turning out to be such a green flag?"

I paused for a second before responding. Me: "Because he is."

Anu: "That's it? No long monologue about his patience, his pasta-making skills, and how he's basically keeping you sane?"

I rolled my eyes but laughed. Me: "You're annoying."

Anu: "And you're in denial. But I'll let it slide. For now."

Just as I was about to close my texts and attempt to clear my head, my phone buzzed again. This time, it was Rishi.

Rishi: "Meet me? Five minutes?"

I blinked at the message, my heart doing that stupid, familiar flip. It had been a while since we'd spent any real time together, with all the studying taking over my life. I hesitated for a second before replying. Me: "Where?"

Rishi: "The usual spot. Ice cream's on me."

A small smile broke across my face. Me: "Fine. But I'm choosing the flavor."

Fifteen minutes later, I was sitting across from Rishi at our favorite ice cream parlor, a shared tub of Belgian choco-chip between us.

"So, how'd it go?" he asked, leaning back in his chair.

I made a face. "Group 1 was okay. Group 2? Let's not talk about it."

He chuckled, shaking his head. "You'll be fine, Aarna. You always are."

"I don't know about that," I muttered, taking a spoonful of ice cream. "Anyway, what's up with you? You never text me out of nowhere like this."

He shrugged. "Thought you could use a break. And some luck before the final exams."

"That's sweet," I admitted, nudging his arm lightly. "Thank you."

"Anytime," he said, his gaze lingering on mine for a second longer than necessary.

The moment passed quickly, but it left me feeling something I didn't have time to process. Because the second I got home, my books were waiting for me, and I had no choice but to dive right back in.

45

AYAAN

The moment I walked out of the exam hall, I knew the paper had been a disaster. Advanced Accounting was a nightmare, but then again, when was it not? I yanked my tie loose and exhaled deeply as I scanned the anxious faces of students exiting the hall. Some looked like they had seen a ghost, while others—those annoying overachievers—seemed to be discussing their answers with an energy I couldn't relate to.

John was waiting outside the center, leaning against his bike, scrolling through his phone. The second he saw me, he smirked.

"How much are you scoring, CA Finalist?" he teased, knowing damn well that I was in no mood for jokes.

I shot him a glare. "Shut up, bro. If I pass this one, I'll personally sponsor your wedding."

He laughed. "That bad?"

"That horrible," I muttered. "I swear, AS 20 EPS made me want to set my answer sheet on fire. Who even cares about earnings per share? I'm not opening a damn stock market."

John chuckled. "You're overreacting. You knew the format, right?"

"Format se kya hoga? (What will format do?) You think the examiner will pass me just because I wrote the damn headings? I swear I saw my soul leave my body after the consolidation question."

John whistled. "Man, even Aarna was stressing about the paper. She left the hall looking like she had just fought in a war."

Hearing her name sent a weird feeling through me, something I wasn't ready to address. I had been spending too much time with her lately, and she had somehow become my person when it came to academics, late-night venting, and life in general.

I checked my phone.

Aarna: I don't think I'm going to pass this paper :((

Aarna: I don't know what to do.

Aarna: Ayaan, are you there?

I sighed. I should have felt bad for her. Maybe I did, somewhere deep inside, but I was already so pissed at how badly my own exam had gone. I didn't have the patience for anyone else's breakdown.

I called her, and the second she picked up, I could hear her sniffling.

"Ayaan... I think I failed," she whispered.

"Aarna, for God's sake, stop being so dramatic."

"Dramatic? Ayaan, I left so many questions! And the ones I attempted were probably wrong. I'm so done," she cried. "I don't think I can do this anymore."

My jaw clenched. "Then don't. Just quit. If you're already this negative, maybe CA isn't for you."

There was a long silence. My own words echoed in my ears, and I knew I had gone too far. But at that moment, I didn't care. I was exhausted, frustrated, and drowning in my own self-doubt.

"Wow," she finally said, her voice hollow. "Thanks, Ayaan. That was really helpful."

"I'm just being realistic," I snapped. "You crying about it won't change your results. Instead of wasting time, maybe start preparing for Law. It's your best subject, right? Or are you going to screw that up too?"

More silence. I could hear her breathing unevenly.

"I shouldn't have called you," she said quietly. And then, the line went dead.

I exhaled sharply and threw my phone into my bag.

John was watching me with a raised eyebrow. "Dude, what the hell was that?"

"Nothing," I muttered, running a hand through my hair.

"That didn't sound like nothing," he pointed out. "You were an ass."

I rolled my eyes. "John, drop it. I'm not in the mood."

"Yeah? Well, neither was she, clearly." He shook his head. "You're pushing her away, you know that, right?"

I scoffed. "She'll be fine. She always is."

But something in my chest felt tight, like I had just messed up in a way I couldn't fix.

I didn't call her back. I didn't apologize. Instead, I focused on Law, ignoring the way my own words kept replaying in my head.

And for the first time in a long time, I hated myself for it.

46

AARNA

The words kept replaying in my head. Over and over again, like a broken record stuck on the cruelest part of a song.

"CA isn't for you."

I had never heard anything so hurtful from Ayaan before. The moment he said it, my heart sank, and now, no matter how hard I tried, I couldn't shake it off. My mind refused to let it go.

Tears pricked at my eyes as I sat on my desk, books open in front of me, but the words were all blurring together. Receivables Management, Amalgamation, Consolidation, AS 20—none of it mattered anymore. My chest tightened with frustration. How could he say that? How could he make me feel like I was nothing after everything we studied together?

A sharp knock on my door pulled me out of my spiral of thoughts. "Come in," I muttered, wiping my face quickly.

Jai walked in, carrying a large cup of coffee in one hand and a mischievous smile on his face. "Guess who brought caffeine and motivation?" he announced, placing the cup on my desk before plopping onto my bed. "Simie told me what happened. Thought I'd drop by and remind you that you're not as useless as your tiny brain is convincing you to be."

I let out a tired sigh, reaching for the coffee. "Jai, it's not just about the exam. Ayaan—he really said some things that hurt. And the worst part is, he's not even sorry for it."

Jai scoffed, shaking his head. "Ayaan is an idiot. You know that, right? Probably overwhelmed with his own stress and decided to be a jerk about it. That doesn't mean what he said is true. You're one of the smartest people I know, Aaru."

"Smart people don't screw up their accounts paper like I did," I muttered, taking a sip of coffee. The warmth helped, but not enough to drown out my self-doubt.

"Oh, please. You think you're the only one? Everyone walked out of that exam looking like they saw their worst nightmare come to life. Trust me, if you found it hard, so did everyone else."

I wanted to believe him, but Ayaan's words had already done their damage. I stayed silent, looking down at my law notes, flipping pages absentmindedly.

Jai leaned forward, snapping his fingers in front of my face. "Okay, listen up. Next paper is law, right? That's your domain. You could answer FEMA questions in your sleep. If there's one thing I know, it's that Aarna is going to ace this exam. So stop moping, and let's do a quick revision before I lose my patience and start dramatically reciting sections from the Bare Act."

I let out a small laugh despite myself. "Fine, fine. Ask me something."

Jai grinned, flipping through my notes before looking up. "Alright, Miss FEMA Expert. Under the Foreign Exchange Management Act, what's the maximum period for realization and repatriation of export proceeds?"

I straightened up. "Nine months from the date of export, except in cases where RBI has permitted a longer period."

"Ding ding ding! Correct answer. See? Your brain still works," Jai said, smirking. "Next question. What are the provisions regarding foreign direct investment under FEMA?"

I leaned back, tapping my fingers against the desk. "Automatic route and government route. Under the automatic route, no prior approval is required from the RBI or the central government. Under the government route, approval from relevant authorities is needed."

"Exactly!" Jai clapped dramatically. "And that, my dear friend, is why you are going to kill it in tomorrow's paper."

I smiled a little. Maybe he was right. Maybe I could push through this, one paper at a time.

The next morning, I walked into the exam hall feeling nervous but ready. The weight of Ayaan's words was still there, lingering like a dull ache, but I refused to let it control me.

The exam began, and as I flipped through the question paper, I felt a wave of relief. It was manageable. I answered FEMA questions with ease, breezed through business law, and made sure my company law answers were structured well.

By the time I walked out, I felt lighter. Not ecstatic, but at least better than I did after accounts.

I didn't call Ayaan that day.

For the first time in weeks, I didn't feel like I needed to.

47

AYAAN

I slammed my pen down as the invigilator announced, "Time's up. Pens down." My law exam had been a disaster. Every question that came up seemed to be the one I had chosen to skip while studying. My brain was fried, my hands ached, and I couldn't shake the sinking feeling in my gut.

As I stepped out of the exam hall, John, my best friend and fellow CA sufferer, caught up to me.

"How was it?" he asked, his expression mirroring my own exhaustion.

"Horrible. I knew I should've revised FEMA better. The MCQs tricked me, and I blanked out in the case law section. What about you?"

John sighed, shoving his hands into his pockets. "Same. FEMA was a nightmare, and don't even get me started on Interpretation of Statutes."

I barely listened, my mind already somewhere else. On her.

Aarna.

I knew she must've done well. Law was her strong suit. Unlike me, she actually enjoyed the subject. And that thought alone made my blood boil.

Just as I pulled out my phone, I saw her name flashing on my screen. Of course. She'd be calling to say her paper went well. That she nailed it while I struggled.

I picked up, my tone sharp. "What?"

"Hey... how was your paper?" she asked, her voice softer than usual.

I let out a humorless chuckle. "Oh, you'd love to know, wouldn't you? Bet you aced it. Meanwhile, I just wasted three hours of my life."

She hesitated. "Ayaan, that's not—"

"You know what? You're a distraction," I snapped, my frustration spilling out. "I spent so much time helping you with accounts, worrying about you, and now look at me. I'm the one failing. I couldn't even focus on tax because of you!"

There was silence on the other end. And then, so quietly I almost didn't hear it, she whispered, "How is this my fault? I never asked you to—"

"Oh, come on, Aarna!" I cut her off. "We both know you're only in my life because you needed help. You were struggling, and I was stupid enough to waste my time on you instead of focusing on myself."

I knew I was being cruel. I knew my words were cutting her, but I didn't stop. My own anger and failure were too much to bear, and she was the easiest person to blame.

She exhaled sharply. "You're saying I was just using you? That all of this was one-sided?" Her voice wavered. "I had feelings for you, Ayaan. And you're telling me I was nothing but a burden?"

I clenched my jaw, but before I could say anything else, I heard it. The tiny, muffled sniffle.

She was crying.

And for some reason, that didn't make me feel guilty. It made me angrier. At her. At myself. At this whole damn thing.

"You know what, Aarna?" I said coldly. "Maybe this was a mistake. You should focus on your exams. And I should focus on mine."

I ended the call before she could respond.

John, who had been watching the whole thing, let out a low whistle. "Damn, dude. That was harsh."

I didn't reply. I just shoved my phone in my pocket and walked away, trying to convince myself that I did the right thing. That Aarna had only been holding me back.

Then why did I feel like absolute shit?

48

AARNA

I stared at the tax paper in front of me, the words blurring together as the weight of everything crashed onto my shoulders. I had prepared for this, I really had, but my mind refused to cooperate. The formulas, the concepts, the case laws I had spent weeks memorizing—they all vanished like smoke.

I felt my hands tremble as I flipped through the pages. The first question itself was a disaster. My pen hovered over the paper, my mind struggling to recall the correct provision. I squeezed my eyes shut, trying to block out the self-doubt creeping in. But it was too late. The words of Ayaan echoed in my head.

"CA isn't for you."

My throat tightened, my eyes burned, but I couldn't afford to cry. Not here. Not in an exam hall full of strangers. I swallowed hard, forcing myself to focus.

You can still fix this. Just breathe.

I skipped the first question and moved on to the second. Something about clubbing of income. It should've been easy. But my mind was still a mess. I scribbled some vague, half-baked answer, hoping for partial marks, but deep down, I knew it wasn't enough.

Halfway through the exam, the dam broke. A tear slipped down my cheek. I quickly wiped it away, but the invigilator had already noticed.

"Are you okay?" she whispered, concern lacing her voice.

I nodded quickly, forcing a weak smile, and turned back to my paper. But my hands were shaking. The numbers blurred, the sections jumbled in my head, and suddenly, it felt like I couldn't breathe.

I shouldn't have let Ayaan's words get to me. I shouldn't have let him make me feel like this. But I did. And now, I was paying the price.

By the time I walked out of the exam hall, I felt completely drained. My body felt heavy, my chest ached from trying to hold back the tears. I saw Anu waiting for me near the gate, her face lighting up when she spotted me. But the moment she saw my expression, her smile faltered.

"Oh no," she said, wrapping an arm around my shoulder. "How bad was it?"

I took a shaky breath. "It was a nightmare. I blanked out. I—I cried during the paper, Anu."

Her eyes widened. "Oh, Aarna..."

"And the worst part?" I let out a humorless laugh. "I know I could've done better if Ayaan hadn't made me feel like absolute shit."

Anu's expression darkened. "What did he do now?"

I shook my head. "It's not even about one thing. It's just... everything. He keeps treating me like I'm some obstacle in his life. And the worst part? I still—" My voice cracked, and I stopped myself.

Anu sighed. "You still like him."

I wiped my face. "Yeah. And I hate that I do."

"You need to stop letting him get to you, Aarna. He's not worth this. No guy is worth this."

I let out a shaky breath, trying to convince myself she was right. But the pain in my chest said otherwise.

ϷϷϷ

That night, as I lay in bed staring at the ceiling, I replayed the exam in my head. The panic, the tears, the regret. I hated feeling this weak. I hated that Ayaan still had this much control over my emotions.

I pulled out my phone and stared at our last conversation. I could text him. Tell him how horrible I felt. Tell him how much he had hurt me. But I knew he wouldn't care.

So instead, I opened Anu's chat.

Aarna: I can't do this anymore.

Anu: Yes, you can. One more group. Just one more.

I took a deep breath. She was right. One more group. One last fight.

Then I could finally be free.

ϷϷϷ

The moment the invigilator placed the costing paper on my desk, I felt my chest tighten. I took a deep breath, convincing myself that I could do this. But the moment I flipped through the pages, panic took over.

The MCQs were tricky, the kind that made you second-guess yourself at every step. I tried to keep my composure, but my mind was blanking out. I marked a few answers with shaky hands, but as I progressed, I found myself crossing them out and changing them repeatedly. Time slipped away, and I hadn't even touched the long questions yet.

Then came the reconciliation of cost books with accounts—a five-mark question that seemed simple at first glance but was anything but. I spent a whole hour on it, redoing the calculations, checking each line, making sure I wasn't missing anything. But every time I thought I had it right, a new discrepancy popped up. My heart pounded louder with each passing minute. An hour gone, just like that. And I still had so much to write.

I rushed through the rest of the paper, scribbling down answers, barely giving myself the time to think. The numbers blurred together, and my mind felt like it was splitting in two—one half trying to solve the problems, the other half screaming at me for wasting so much time. When the final bell rang, my hands were still moving, trying to finish the last calculation. The invigilator pulled the paper from my grasp, and I sat there, frozen, watching my incomplete answers disappear with it.

I walked out of the exam hall in a daze, my eyes already welling up with tears. My head was spinning, my throat tight with the effort of holding back sobs. This wasn't how it was supposed to go. I had studied so hard. I had sacrificed so much sleep. And yet, it still wasn't enough.

And then I saw him.

Ayaan.

Laughing, high-fiving John, looking so carefree, as if today's paper had been a walk in the park for him. His face was beaming with confidence, and the sight of it made my stomach churn. I stood there, feeling utterly shattered, while he stood just a few feet away, celebrating like nothing had happened.

I turned away before he could see me. I didn't want him to look at me—not now, not when I was a complete mess. My chest felt tight as I searched for someone familiar, someone who could make me feel less alone. And then I spotted Anu, standing a few steps ahead, scrolling through her phone.

I rushed to her, my vision blurring as the tears I had tried to hold back spilled over. "Anu," I choked out, and she looked up instantly.

Her face softened. "Aarna... oh god, what happened?"

I wiped at my face aggressively, but the tears kept falling. "It was bad. It was so bad."

She put her arm around me and guided me toward a quieter corner. "Okay, breathe. What happened?"

I took a shuddering breath. "I blanked out during the MCQs. They were so confusing. And that reconciliation question? I wasted a whole hour on it. My paper was so lengthy, I couldn't even finish it properly."

Anu frowned. "That question was tough, yeah, but you must have done okay in the rest of the paper, right?"

I shook my head violently. "No. I rushed through everything. And then when I walked out, I saw Ayaan... he was celebrating. Like today was just another win for him."

Anu's face darkened slightly. "Aarna... you know how he is. He's probably just happy his own paper went well. It doesn't mean—"

"I don't care what it means," I snapped, wiping my nose with my sleeve. "I just... I feel like shit, Anu. I feel like I don't belong here. I feel like no matter how hard I try, it's never enough."

Anu's grip on my shoulder tightened. "Aarna, stop. You belong here just as much as anyone else. And I swear, if Ayaan's words are still messing with your head, you need to let that go. He has no right to make you feel like this."

I nodded weakly, but deep inside, I knew it wasn't that easy. His words—his cold, sharp words—were still echoing in my mind. 'CA isn't for you.' The worst part? A tiny part of me believed him.

Anu sighed and gave me a tight hug. "Go home, take a shower, eat something good, and sleep. Your brain needs a reset before the next exam."

I nodded again, but my hands were still shaking. The exhaustion, the disappointment, the self-doubt—it all weighed me down like an anchor. I needed to let it go, but I didn't know how.

All I knew was that I had another exam to prepare for. And despite everything, I had to keep going.

49

AYAAN

The last paper was finally over. As I walked out of the exam hall, a strange mix of relief and exhaustion settled over me. The past month had been nothing short of a battlefield, and yet, deep down, I knew I had done enough to clear this attempt. Maybe not with flying colors, but enough to get through.

John clapped me on the back as we exited the center. "Man, it's over. Can you believe it?" He let out a long breath, stretching his arms above his head. "No more waking up at 4 a.m. to study. No more damn taxation theories and reconciliation statements. We are free!"

I chuckled, shaking my head. "You do realize we have to start preparing for finals soon, right? This was just the beginning."

John groaned. "Why do you have to ruin every happy moment? Let me at least enjoy today."

I smirked but didn't respond. The truth was, I wasn't in the mood to celebrate. Not when I knew Aarna was still struggling. The thought of her clouded my mind. I had been avoiding her since the last fight, since I told her she was a distraction.

I knew I had been harsh. Too harsh. But I couldn't bring myself to take it back. She was already so emotionally invested, and I had no room for that kind of attachment. I had my own battles to fight, my own ambitions to chase.

As we walked toward the main gate, I spotted her from a distance. She was standing with Anu and Simie, her face pale, her eyes swollen. She looked completely drained, holding onto her bag like it was the only thing keeping her upright. I could tell from the way she clutched her water bottle that she had cried again.

I exhaled sharply, forcing myself to look away.

"Dude, you should talk to her," John muttered beside me, noticing my glance. "You were way too harsh the other day."

"She'll be fine," I said, my voice colder than I intended. "She needs to learn how to handle shit on her own. I can't be responsible for her."

John raised an eyebrow. "You do realize she cared about you, right? Like, really cared. And you just..." He shook his head. "Forget it, man. Do whatever you want."

His words gnawed at me, but I pushed the guilt away. I didn't ask her to fall for me. I never promised her anything. If she was hurting now, it wasn't my fault. She should have known better.

I felt my phone vibrate in my pocket. A message from my mom: Come home soon, beta. We're proud of you.

Proud. The word stung a little. If they knew the kind of person I had become over the past few months, would they still be proud?

"Let's get out of here," I muttered, stepping away. I didn't look back at Aarna. I couldn't afford to.

50

I stared at my phone screen for a long minute, reading Ayaan's message over and over again.

"Come over. Bring my sweatshirt."

I could feel my hands tremble as I stood outside Ayaan's apartment, his sweatshirt clutched in my hands like a goodbye letter I never wanted to write. I knew what this meant. He wanted his things back. He wanted to close this chapter, erase whatever we had shared, and I was just supposed to accept it.

I knocked on the door, my heart pounding so hard it echoed in my ears. Within seconds, he opened it, his eyes meeting mine with an unreadable expression. He looked tired, maybe even regretful, but that didn't change the reality of why I was here.

"You actually came," he said, voice softer than I expected.

"You asked me to," I replied, lifting the sweatshirt slightly. He took it from my hands but didn't move aside, didn't let me in. For a second, I thought that was it. That he'd say thank you and close the door, leaving me standing there with nothing but the weight of everything I wished had gone differently.

But then he pulled me inside.

I barely had a second to process before his lips crashed against mine, stealing my breath and all the thoughts I had prepared for this moment. I gasped, my fingers gripping his shirt for support, but I didn't pull away. I didn't want to. His hands were on my waist, gripping me like he was afraid I'd disappear, and maybe I should have. Maybe I should have said no, stepped back, reminded myself of all the pain he had caused me in the last few weeks.

But I didn't.

I kissed him back, harder, deeper, desperate to understand what this meant. Was this an apology? Was this closure? Or was this something real—something that hadn't shattered despite everything?

His hands roamed up my sides, fingers brushing under my shirt, the warmth of his touch sending a shiver down my spine. My back hit the wall as his lips moved to my jaw, then my neck, each kiss leaving a trail of fire on my skin. My breath hitched as he nipped at the sensitive spot beneath my ear, his body pressing against mine, his heartbeat as erratic as my own.

"Ayaan," I whispered, barely recognizing my own voice.

He hummed against my skin, his hands sliding under my shirt, fingers warm and rough against my bare waist. My pulse raced as he traced lazy circles over my skin, setting it ablaze with every movement. I felt dizzy, intoxicated by the way he touched me, by the way I let him. My hands tangled in his hair, tugging him closer, needing more, needing to believe that this was real.

His fingers skimmed higher, pushing my shirt up inch by inch, his lips never leaving my skin. The air between us was thick, charged with something I couldn't name. His hands moved to my hips, gripping them firmly before pulling me closer, eliminating the last sliver of space between us.

I let out a shaky breath as his lips captured mine again, this time slower, deeper, his tongue teasing mine as if he wanted to savor every second. His hands moved down, over the curve of my thighs, lifting me effortlessly as I wrapped my legs around his waist. He carried me across the room, his lips never leaving mine, until I felt the cool surface of his bed beneath me.

"Ayaan..." I whispered again, this time unsure, but he silenced me with another kiss, his hands exploring, caressing, memorizing. My own hands mirrored his movements, running over his chest, tracing the lines of his toned body, feeling the way he shuddered beneath my touch.

The room was a blur of heat and hushed breaths, of tangled limbs and whispered names. Every touch, every kiss, every sigh pulled me deeper into him, into the moment, making me forget everything else.

I knew I should stop. I knew I should think. But I didn't want to.

I wanted to believe that this was real. That we weren't just something temporary. That when the morning came, he wouldn't look at me like a mistake.

So I let myself fall, let myself get lost in him, in the way he made me feel like I was the only thing that mattered in that moment.

Because for the first time in weeks, I didn't feel broken.

I felt wanted.

51

❦

AYAAN

The moment she was in my arms, I knew there was no turning back. Aarna was intoxicating—her warmth, her trust, the way her lips parted slightly as she gazed up at me. She had no idea what she was stepping into, no idea of the hunger I had suppressed for so long.

I trailed my fingers along her jawline, tilting her chin up, watching her shudder at my touch. "You're beautiful," I murmured, letting my eyes devour every inch of her. The soft glow of the dim room highlighted the curves I longed to claim, and as I traced slow, deliberate patterns against her skin, she melted under me, surrendering to the heat between us.

Aarna's breath hitched as I slid my hands down her sides, exploring, owning, marking. My lips trailed along her collarbone, my teeth grazing just enough to make her gasp. The way she responded, the way her fingers gripped my arms—it only fueled the fire burning inside me.

She let me take her, let me lose myself in her, let me pull her into my world of darkness and desire. Her moans were soft, hesitant at times, but never resisting. She let me take control, let me taste every inch of her, and when she clung to me, whispering my name, I felt it—power, raw and consuming.

But then, there was a shift. A subtle moment where she breathed, "Ayaan... stop."

I couldn't. Not yet.

I held her wrists above her head, murmuring against her lips, "Just a little more." My voice was rough, desperate. I knew I was pushing, I knew she was starting to waver, but I needed this. I needed all of her. My grip tightened as I took exactly what I wanted, what I craved. And she let me. She always let me.

When it was over, silence stretched between us, thick and suffocating. Aarna sat up, reaching for her clothes, her hands shaking just slightly. I watched her, leaning back against the pillow, my heart still pounding from the high. She avoided my gaze, and I knew—she was already regretting this.

"What does this mean?" she finally asked, her voice barely above a whisper.

I exhaled, running a hand through my hair, knowing this moment would come. I looked at her—disheveled, vulnerable, waiting. And yet, I couldn't give her what she wanted.

"It was just a one-time thing," I said, voice void of any emotion.

She froze. I saw the flicker of pain in her eyes before she looked away, blinking rapidly.

"Right," she whispered, her voice cracking. She turned away from me, hastily dressing, but I could see her wiping at her cheeks, her breaths uneven.

A flicker of guilt twisted in my chest. It was faint, barely there, but enough to remind me that I had broken something in her tonight.

I should say something. Anything. But I didn't.

Instead, I watched as she collected herself, avoiding my eyes one last time before slipping out of the room, leaving behind only the scent of her skin and the ghost of her touch.

And as much as I had told myself this was nothing, I knew—I would remember the way she looked at me before she walked away forever.

52

AARNA

I stepped out of Ayaan's house, my mind swirling with a mixture of confusion and hurt. The person I had just encountered felt nothing like the Ayaan I had always known. He had been my greenest flag—kind, understanding, patient. And yet, the way he had spoken to me just now, the cold detachment in his voice, had sent an unsettling chill through my bones. Even Anu had been left speechless, her usual lively self replaced by a stunned silence.

As I walked away, I instinctively reached for my phone, my fingers moving on autopilot to open Snapchat. My heart sank the moment I typed his name into the search bar—his Bitmoji was gone. The little ghost next to his name, which had always signified our streak, had disappeared. My breath hitched as realization dawned—he had blocked me.

A lump formed in my throat, but I quickly switched to WhatsApp. Maybe he had just logged out or deactivated his Snapchat. Maybe this was a mistake. But as I searched for his name, all I saw was a single gray tick next to our last message. My profile picture and status were missing from his end. My hands began to tremble as I tried Instagram next. But no, he wasn't there either. Ayaan had wiped me out of his digital world completely.

My stomach churned as I exited the app and, with a flicker of desperation, opened my SMS inbox. And there it was.

Goodbye Aarna, I really need to focus on my life right now and cannot afford any distraction at this point.

My vision blurred. The words on the screen didn't feel real. Goodbye? As if I was someone to be left behind, discarded like an old chapter of his life? A distraction?

A sharp pang shot through my chest, my breaths coming in quick, uneven gasps. The cab ride back home became a blur, the city lights flashing past in a haze of color, but all I could hear was the deafening sound of my own heartbeat. My hands felt clammy, my head light. The walls of the cab seemed to close in around me, and I struggled to catch my breath.

I needed air. I needed to calm down. But I couldn't.

Ayaan was gone. Just like that.

Panic clawed at my throat, my fingers gripping the edge of the seat as I tried to steady myself. I gasped for air, but it felt like I was suffocating. My pulse raced, my ears rang. My body refused to listen to me. My mind screamed at me to hold it together, but the weight in my chest only grew heavier.

I don't know how I made it home. The moment the cab stopped in front of my building, I fumbled with the door handle, my movements shaky. I threw a couple of bills at the driver and stumbled out, barely hearing his concerned "Miss, are you okay?" before I turned away.

I needed my bed. I needed silence. I needed this all to stop spinning.

Pushing open the door to my house, I ignored the distant chatter of my family in the living room. I didn't stop to acknowledge my mom's voice calling my name. I didn't want to answer questions. I didn't want to talk. I just wanted to disappear into my room, into the comforting embrace of my blanket, and pretend for a few hours that this wasn't happening.

I slipped into bed, curled into myself, and shut my eyes tightly. Maybe if I slept, this nightmare would fade. Maybe when I woke up, Ayaan would still be my greenest flag, the same boy who had once made me feel safe.

But deep down, I knew.

Some things, once broken, could never be the same again.

ᗑᗑᗑ

RESULT DAY

The house was filled with an electric buzz of excitement and anticipation. My desk was surrounded by Simie, Jai, and my family, all eagerly waiting for me to check my CA Intermediate results. Their voices blended together, a mix of cheers and encouragement, but my head was drowning in a sea of doubts.

My hands trembled as I typed in my roll number. The captcha felt like a cruel joke, forcing me to slow down and take in every agonizing second before hitting the submit button. A deep breath, a final hesitation, and then—I pressed enter.

The screen loaded.

Unsuccessful.

The word sat there, staring back at me, taunting me. Not once, but twice. Both groups—failed.

The noise around me faded. My heartbeat echoed in my ears, my chest tightening as the weight of failure settled over me like a suffocating blanket. My fingers hovered over the keyboard, as if refreshing the page would change the outcome. But nothing changed. It was real.

I had failed.

Everything blurred. The voices, the cheers, the presence of my friends—it all became distant. I felt lost, broken, as if the ground beneath me had disappeared. I had given my all, poured every ounce of effort into this exam, and still, it hadn't been enough.

Simie's hand found mine, her grip tightening in silent support. Jai's usual confident voice softened as he called my name, but I couldn't bring myself to respond. I could barely breathe past the lump in my throat.

And then, the final blow.

My phone buzzed. A message from Somya.

"Ayaan cleared."

Ayaan had passed. Of course, he had. My grip on my phone tightened as another message popped up.

"Kaira passed too."

My stomach twisted painfully. I swallowed back the burn rising in my throat. One after another, everyone was moving forward, and I was stuck. Left behind.

Another ping.

"Anu and I couldn't clear."

A sharp exhale left my lips. I wasn't alone. But it didn't lessen the ache. It didn't erase the sinking feeling that everything was going against me.

Tears pricked my eyes, but I refused to let them fall. Not here. Not in front of everyone.

I forced a shaky breath and slowly shut my laptop. My world had just turned upside down, but outside of me, life was moving on. I wasn't ready to face it. Not yet.

53

AYAAN

The moment my result flashed on the screen, a surge of euphoria washed over me. I had passed. I had actually cleared both groups of my CA Intermediate exams. A wide grin spread across my face as the reality of it sank in. This was everything I had worked for.

My house erupted in celebrations. My parents were beaming with pride, relatives calling in to congratulate me, sweets being distributed, and laughter echoing through the walls. The weight of all those sleepless nights, the stress, the fear—it had all been worth it.

But amidst the joy, there was a dull ache in my chest. John and Somya hadn't cleared. Their names were missing from the list of successful candidates. I had seen Somya's message right after checking my results, a simple 'Couldn't clear. Congrats to you, though.' It didn't sit right with me. I wanted to celebrate, but knowing that two of my closest friends were struggling made it bittersweet.

Later in the evening, Somya dropped by. The moment she stepped into my house, she gave me a weak smile, her eyes betraying her disappointment.

"Congrats, Ayaan," she said, handing me a small box of chocolates.

"You really didn't have to," I replied, accepting it anyway.

She shrugged. "I wanted to." Her eyes wandered over the decorations, the happy chatter in the background. "Big celebration, huh?"

I nodded. "Yeah, it's a big deal." I hesitated for a moment before adding, "I'm really sorry, Somya. I know how much this meant to you. And John too."

She sighed. "It is what it is. I'll try again. But that's not why I'm here."

I raised an eyebrow. "Then what?"

Somya's expression turned serious as she crossed her arms. "I need to ask you something. Why did you behave like such a jerk to Aarna?"

I exhaled sharply, rolling my eyes. "Not this again."

"Yes, this again," she snapped. "What was that all about? Blocking her everywhere? Ignoring her like she didn't exist?"

I scoffed. "Does it even matter anymore? I don't care, Somya. I have a life to build."

"Ayaan, she cared about you. And you just cut her off like that? What the hell?"

Something in me flared up at that. "Oh, she cared about me? Right. That's why when I had feelings for her, she went to prom with Rishi."

Somya's eyes widened. "Are you serious right now? She asked you first, Ayaan! And you said no. That's why she went with Rishi."

My jaw tightened. "Doesn't matter. She still went. And honestly? I don't give a damn anymore."

Somya studied me for a moment before shaking her head. "You're impossible. I don't want to get in between all this, but you should know, Aarna was really hurt."

A bitter laugh escaped my lips. "Hurt? Good. Maybe this is karma. Maybe she deserved to fail."

Somya's expression darkened. "Wow. That's low, even for you."

I shrugged, smirking. "Say what you want. I'm done caring."

Somya stared at me for a few seconds before letting out a sigh. "You know what, Ayaan? I really hope you figure yourself out before it's too late."

She turned on her heel and walked away, leaving me standing there, the celebrations around me feeling oddly distant.

54

AARNA

I never thought I'd feel this kind of clarity again. It's strange how people—situations—can break you down to your rawest form, but somehow, life finds a way to build you back up, stronger and sharper than before.

When I met Apurva, I was at my lowest. She was my senior in school, someone I had admired from a distance back then, but never really spoken to. She had cleared CA Intermediate this attempt, the very thing I had failed. Yet, there was no arrogance in her, no distance between us. Just warmth, understanding, and the kind of energy I needed.

We clicked instantly. It wasn't forced, nor was it something I actively sought. It just happened. Like the universe was throwing me a lifeline in the form of a friend who had walked this road before me.

Days started looking different. Instead of wallowing in my failure, I channeled everything into discipline. I mapped out a study plan, scheduling my days around lectures and practice exams. But this time, I wasn't just studying—I was taking care of myself too.

Fitness became a newfound love. Every morning, Apurva and I went for runs, breathing in the crisp air, letting the rhythm of our steps drown out the noise of self-doubt. The first few days were brutal—legs sore, lungs burning—but soon, I started enjoying it. Feeling my body get stronger gave me the kind of confidence I hadn't felt in a long time. It was as if I was slowly reclaiming myself, piece by piece.

Food, sleep, routine—everything became intentional. No more sleepless nights spent overthinking, no more endless scrolling through social media, stalking people who had already left my life. The moment I decided to focus on me, everything else became background noise.

Even Ayaan.

I saw him outside college once, standing with his friends, laughing about something. The old me would have felt something—anger, sadness, maybe even regret. But that day, I felt nothing. No sting in my chest, no bitterness, no longing. Just... indifference.

And that was the biggest victory of all.

For the first time in a long time, I wasn't looking back. I wasn't waiting for apologies, explanations, or closure. I had given myself the closure I needed. I had built a world where I didn't need people who didn't value me.

I had one goal now—to clear CA Intermediate. Not to prove anything to anyone, not to outshine anyone else, but for myself. Because I deserved success, and I was going to make sure I earned it.

Apurva and I sat together in the library every evening, solving mock tests, exchanging notes, discussing doubts. She was my rock, my motivation, my reminder that this could be done. Every time I faltered, she reminded me that failing once didn't define me—getting back up did.

This attempt was going to be different. Not just because I was preparing better, but because I was different. Stronger.

Wiser. More in control of my own life.

And for the first time in forever, I knew—I was going to be okay.

ᐯᐯᐯ

I had deleted Instagram at the start of my exam prep. No distractions, no mindless scrolling—just me, my books, and my daily routine. It was easier this way, keeping my head clear, focusing on what mattered.

Simie, of course, thought I was crazy. "Just log in for five minutes. At least check the group chat," she had said multiple times, but I always shook my head.

Tonight, as I was highlighting my notes, my phone buzzed. Simie's name flashed on the screen.

"Hey, what's up?" I answered, still underlining a formula.

"You really have no clue, do you?" she asked, amusement lacing her tone.

I sighed. "About what?"

"Rishi's dating someone."

My pen hovered mid-air. "Okay."

Simie paused. "That's it? Just 'okay'?"

I capped my pen. "Yeah. Who is it?"

"Hima. She lives in his building. Apparently, they started talking a while ago, and now it's official."

I let her words settle, waiting for something—anything—to shift inside me. But there was nothing. No sudden pang in my chest, no tightness in my throat.

"Simie?" I said after a moment.

"Yeah?"

"Did you call just to tell me this?"

"Well... yeah," she admitted. "I mean, you two have a history. I thought you'd—"

"Simie," I cut her off, flipping the page in my textbook, "I really don't care."

She went quiet for a few seconds. "Seriously?"

"Seriously."

It wasn't a lie. I wasn't pretending. I was just... done. Maybe at one point, this news would've ruined my day, sent me spiraling into overthinking, but not anymore. Rishi and I had already drifted apart. This was just proof that it was time to close whatever chapter we had left.

I picked up my pen again. "I need to study. Exams start next week."

Simie sighed. "Fine, Miss Cold-Hearted. But don't say I didn't tell you."

I chuckled. "Noted. Bye, Simie."

Hanging up, I glanced at my phone for a second before setting it face down. My world hadn't shattered. My heart hadn't ached.

I had books to read, goals to achieve.

And that's exactly what I was going to do.

55

RISHI

I never thought about what love should feel like. I just assumed when it happened, it would be unmistakable. That being with someone meant something, that crossing lines brought clarity.

But with Hima, it didn't.

We had been together for months now. We had spent nights whispering over the phone, sharing secrets, going further than I had before. But even with all that—especially with all that—it felt like I was searching for something I couldn't name. And no matter how close I got, I never really found it.

Because she wasn't Aarna.

I sighed, staring at my phone. I hadn't spoken to Aarna in weeks. She had shut herself off from everything, deleted Instagram, stopped picking up unnecessary calls, throwing herself into exam prep. If it were anyone else, I'd call it overkill. But this was Aarna.

And I missed her.

Before I could think twice, I grabbed my jacket and my keys. The streets were quieter than usual, a chill settling in the evening air. Aarna's building wasn't far from mine, but every step felt heavier than it should.

When I reached, I hesitated outside the gate, fingers curling and uncurling. She might not want to see me. But I needed to see her.

I dialed her number. It rang twice before she picked up.

"Hello?" Her voice was softer than I remembered, like she'd just woken up from a long nap.

"Hey," I said, forcing my voice to stay steady. "Can you come down for a minute?"

A beat of silence. Then, "Rishi, it's late."

"I know. Just—please."

Another pause, then a quiet sigh. "Fine. Five minutes."

I exhaled, relieved. Leaning against the cold metal gate, I waited, my heart beating just a little faster than it should.

56

AARNA

The air outside was crisp, the night carrying the faint scent of damp earth. I tightened my shawl around me as I stepped through the gate, my breath visible in the cold air. Rishi stood there, hands buried in his jacket pockets, looking at me like he hadn't seen me in years.

Something about the way he looked at me—soft yet searching—unraveled something deep inside.

"I didn't think you'd come," I said, my voice quieter than I intended.

He exhaled a small laugh, tilting his head. "You always say that, but you always do."

I shouldn't have come. I knew that. And yet, here I was, standing before him, feeling exposed in a way that had nothing to do with the cold.

He looked the same, but he didn't feel the same. Maybe it was the weight of unspoken words between us, or maybe it was just me, cracking when I thought I had hardened.

"So, what's up?" I asked, trying to sound indifferent.

"Just... wanted to see you before your exams," he said, eyes searching mine for something even I wasn't sure of.

I nodded, hugging myself a little tighter.

Silence stretched between us, thick with something I didn't want to name. I should've been fine. I had convinced myself that I had moved on, that I was past this. Past him. But standing here, under the dull glow of the streetlight, I wasn't sure of anything anymore.

I hated how easily he made me feel like this—vulnerable, unsteady, as if one wrong move would make everything collapse.

"I should go," I whispered, taking a small step back.

He opened his mouth as if to say something, but then closed it, nodding. "Yeah. Okay."

I turned and walked away before I could change my mind. Each step felt heavier than the last.

Back in my room, I pulled out my notes on Registration of Charges in Law, forcing my focus onto legal provisions, documentation requirements—anything that would drown out the lingering weight of his presence.

I willed myself not to think of how he made me feel. Not to wonder if he felt even a fraction of the same.

And eventually, exhaustion won. Sleep took over, but even in my dreams, I wasn't sure if I had truly escaped him.

57

RISHI

Ending things with Hima was easier than I expected. Maybe because I had known, deep down, that it was inevitable. She deserved someone who looked at her and felt certain, someone who didn't have ghosts lingering in his heart. And I wasn't that person.

She didn't cry. She didn't even ask why. She just nodded, exhaled, and said, "I had a feeling this was coming."

There was something strange about breaking up with someone you had been close to, but never truly connected with. It felt like walking away from a house you had never really lived in—a structure without a home inside. And yet, despite the lack of pain, there was an emptiness that I couldn't quite name.

I threw myself into CFA prep. The moment I cracked open the first book, a wave of urgency hit me. This was my future. The world of numbers, risk assessments, financial forecasting—it demanded precision, clarity, discipline. It wasn't something you half-heartedly pursued.

At first, it worked. I buried myself in coursework, mock tests, and revision plans. But no matter how much I tried to drown myself in calculations, my thoughts drifted elsewhere.

To her.

Aarna.

I checked in on her now and then—small, casual texts asking how her exams were going, if she was sleeping enough, if she had eaten properly. She replied with brief, polite responses, never indulging me beyond necessity. And yet, I kept checking.

I told myself it was just concern, just habit. But I knew better. I knew what it meant when my eyes instinctively searched for her name in my contacts, when I reread old messages I had no reason to look at.

She was everywhere and nowhere at the same time. In the silence between my study sessions, in the spaces between my thoughts. And I hated how easily she still had that power over me.

One evening, after a long study session, I found myself staring at my phone, my fingers hovering over her name. I wanted to say something. Ask her if she was okay. Tell her I missed her. But what would be the point?

I sighed, setting my phone down and running a hand through my hair.

I had ended things with Hima, but the real problem wasn't my relationship with her. It was the one I had never fully let go of.

Aarna had always been my unfinished sentence. And I didn't know how to end it—or if I even wanted to.

58

AARNA

The moment I walked out of the exam hall, I knew it.

I had done it.

Every calculation, every case law, every principle I had drilled into my brain over the past months had flowed effortlessly onto the paper. It was as if my mind had finally found its rhythm, and for the first time in a long time, I felt an unshakable certainty settle inside me. I was going to clear this attempt.

As I stepped into the cool evening air, I exhaled a breath I hadn't realized I'd been holding. The weight of endless late nights, countless cups of coffee, and pages upon pages of notes lifted from my shoulders.

And in that moment, I knew exactly what I wanted to do next.

ppp

I pulled out my phone and without overthinking it, I sent Rishi a message.

Me: Free tomorrow night? Let's go on a real date this time.

A few seconds later, my phone buzzed.

Rishi: A date? With me? Wow, someone's feeling confident after acing their exams. Where to, madam?

Me: Nori. It's a new Thai place. Don't complain.

Rishi: Avocado sushi?

Me: Obviously.

Rishi: Okay. Pick you up at 7.

I smiled, shaking my head. This was happening. It was finally happening.

The next evening, I found myself seated across from Rishi in a cozy corner of Nori, the dimly lit ambiance wrapping around us like a quiet cocoon. The scent of soy, sesame, and chili filled the air as we skimmed the menu, though we already knew what we wanted.

"Avocado sushi and chili noodles," I told the waiter with a small smile.

Rishi leaned back in his chair, studying me. "So, this is an actual date, huh?"

I looked up at him, my fingers tracing the rim of my glass. "Yeah. I think it's about time."

His gaze softened, and for a moment, neither of us spoke.

The food arrived, and as we started eating, the conversation naturally deepened. We talked about my exam—how I was finally free, how I knew I had given it my best shot. And then, almost as if the words had been waiting for the right moment, I told him about Ayaan.

I spoke about the pain, the confusion, the way I had built walls around myself because of it. I told him things I hadn't even fully admitted to myself before, letting my words fall into the space between us.

Rishi listened. Really listened. And when I was done, he reached across the table, his fingers brushing against mine before finally wrapping around my hand. His touch was warm, grounding.

"Aarna," he said softly, "you deserved better."

I swallowed, nodding.

He gave my hand a light squeeze, his eyes holding a quiet reassurance. "And I hope you know that now."

I smiled, feeling something settle inside me. "I do."

Then, just when the moment felt too heavy, he smirked. "You know, if this was a movie, this would be the part where I say something profound and kiss you."

I rolled my eyes. "Good thing this isn't a movie."

He gasped dramatically. "Excuse me? My lines are wasted on you."

I laughed, shaking my head, and for the first time in a long time, I felt light.

Maybe, just maybe, this was exactly where I was meant to be.

59

RISHI

When Aarna stepped into Nori that evening, I swear the world around me blurred.

When Aarna walked into Nori, every breath in my lungs stilled.

Her dress—black, sleek, and sinfully tight—clung to her curves like it had been stitched onto her skin, sculpting her in a way that left little to the imagination. The fabric shimmered subtly under the dim lights, emphasizing the elegant lines of her body as she moved. The deep neckline plunged just enough to make my throat tighten, while the thin straps framed her bare shoulders, leaving them exposed like an invitation I wasn't sure I had the strength to resist.

The dress had a teasing cutout at her waist, just beneath her ribs, revealing a sliver of her smooth, golden skin. It was maddening—the contrast of the modest midi length and the bold, daring slit that ran up her thigh, showing just enough with every step to leave me completely wrecked.

Her hair, dark and glossy, cascaded in soft waves down her back, framing her face in a way that was both effortless and devastating. A few loose strands fell over her cheek, making her look impossibly alluring, like she had walked straight out of a dream meant to destroy me. Her makeup was sharp—kohl-lined eyes that smoldered with intensity, long lashes that cast delicate shadows against her skin, and lips painted a muted red, the kind that made my gaze keep dipping to her mouth every time she spoke.

She carried a designer purse, small and sleek, hanging from her wrist with effortless grace. It was an extension of her—elegant, refined, yet exuding silent power. And then there were her heels. Jet black, pointed, with thin straps wrapping around her ankles. They gave her a few extra inches, making her legs look impossibly long, yet she still barely reached my shoulders. It was unfair, really, how someone could be so tiny and yet hold this much power over me.

And then... her eyes.

God, those eyes.

Dark, knowing, filled with something unreadable that made me feel like I was standing under a microscope, every thought in my head laid bare before her. They flicked over me once, slow and deliberate, before she arched a brow, almost like she could sense my unraveling.

She wore subtle jewelry—a delicate silver chain that rested just above her collarbones, tiny diamond studs that caught the light, and bracelets that jingled softly whenever she moved her wrist. But the thing that destroyed me the most? The anklet.

The same one I had given her years ago.

It glimmered softly against her skin, a quiet reminder of something I wasn't sure I still had the right to claim.

And as she stood there, completely composed while I fought for a single coherent thought, I knew one thing for certain—Aarna had never looked more dangerous.

Or more like mine.

She wore black heels, sharp and sleek, elongating her already toned legs, adding a few inches to her height. Yet even with them, she barely reached my shoulder. It was unfair, the way she looked—like she had stepped out of a dream designed specifically to wreck me.

"Hey," she greeted, her voice smooth and composed, yet carrying a quiet warmth.

"Hey," I echoed, my voice oddly rough.

We clicked a lot of photos together, capturing the moment as if we both knew it was something we'd want to hold onto. Every time I looked at her through the lens, she seemed to glow in a way that made my chest tighten. When she wasn't looking, I pulled out a small bouquet of orchids I had brought for her, watching as her eyes widened in pleasant surprise.

"You got me flowers?" she asked, her fingers brushing over the petals.

I shrugged. "You deserve them."

She looked at me for a beat longer than necessary before tucking a loose strand of hair behind her ear.

The server arrived with our orders—avocado sushi and spicy chili noodles. The warm aroma of Thai spices filled the air as we dug in, savoring the flavors between sips of lemon iced tea. Conversation flowed easily, shifting between lighthearted banter and unspoken emotions lingering between us.

But the evening took a sharp turn when she started talking about Ayaan. I listened in silence, feeling something dark unfurl inside me. Every detail, every ounce of pain in her voice made my grip tighten on the table edge. She spoke with composure, but I could hear the weight behind her words.

I should've been there. I should have stuck by her, fought for her, never let her go through that alone. And now, knowing what she had been through, all I could think about was finding Ayaan and making him regret ever breathing in the same space as her.

I clenched my jaw. "I swear to God, Aarna, if I ever see him, I'll—"

She placed her hand over mine, firm but calm. "Rishi."

My eyes snapped to hers, burning with anger, but she only shook her head, her grip tightening. "The past doesn't matter anymore. The future does."

I swallowed the lump in my throat, staring at her. Her eyes held nothing but certainty, an unshakable strength that both calmed and infuriated me at the same time.

After a long pause, I nodded. "Fine."

She smiled then, a small but real one, and gestured towards the menu. "Now, let's order dessert before you actually go looking for a fight."

A chuckle slipped past my lips, and just like that, the heavy moment melted away. We ended up sharing a plate of matcha cheesecake, laughing about old memories, arguing over which of us looked better in the photos, and savoring every bit of the night. She was laughing at one of my stupid jokes, tilting her head back slightly, and in that moment, I realized how much I had missed this. Missed her.

For the first time in a long time, it felt right. It felt like home.

60

AARNA

61

RISHI

The weight of the CFA Level One exam had been pressing down on me for months, and the moment I walked out of the exam hall, a wave of relief crashed over me. It was done. I had given it my best, and now, for the first time in what felt like forever, I could breathe again. But even in that moment of triumph, my mind wasn't on the results. It was on her.

Aarna.

I had been waiting for this—waiting to finally ask her, officially, to be mine. No more blurred lines, no more uncertainty. Just us.

That evening, I set up the perfect setting. I reserved a private rooftop at one of the finest restaurants in the city, a place with fairy lights woven between vines, the soft glow of candles flickering against the glass railing, and a view that stretched out over the skyline. I wanted the night to feel magical, like the beginning of something new and beautiful.

I arrived early, making sure every detail was perfect—the bouquet of red and white roses on the table, the soft acoustic music playing in the background, the wine chilled just right. And then, I waited.

When she finally arrived, dressed in a stunning emerald green dress that flowed with her every movement, I forgot how to breathe. Her hair cascaded down her back, loose waves framing her delicate features. She was a vision, an ethereal kind of beauty that made everything else fade away.

"A rooftop dinner?" she teased, her eyes scanning the setup. "Rishi, this is... beautiful."

I pulled out her chair, watching the way her lips curved into a smile as she sat down. "Only the best for you."

The evening was effortless. We talked, we laughed, we stole glances that said more than words ever could. And then, as the night deepened and the city lights twinkled beneath us, I reached across the table, taking her hand in mine.

"Aarna," I started, my voice steady but my heart hammering in my chest. "We've been through so much together. And after everything, there's one thing I'm absolutely sure of—I want you. Not just in passing, not just as a memory. I want you with me, in every way that matters."

Her breath hitched, her fingers tightening slightly around mine.

I pulled out a small velvet box and placed it in front of her—not a ring, not yet, but a delicate silver bracelet with a tiny charm shaped like an infinity symbol. "This is my way of asking—will you be mine?"

She stared at the bracelet, then at me, her eyes glistening under the golden lights. A slow, breathtaking smile spread across her lips before she nodded. "Yes, Rishi. A thousand times yes."

Relief, joy, something deeper than happiness settled in my chest as I stood, pulling her into my arms. And then, I kissed her—slow, deep, with every ounce of feeling I had kept bottled up for so long. The city hummed around us, but in that moment, all I knew was her.

And just like that, she was mine.

179

62

AARNA

The morning of my CA Inter results was a blur of nerves and rituals. I woke up before sunrise, my heart thudding like a drum against my ribs. This was it—the day that could shape my future, the day I had worked tirelessly for, the day that held the power to validate every late-night study session, every sacrificed plan, and every ounce of stress I had endured.

Slipping into my lucky outfit—a simple navy-blue kurti and white leggings, the same ones I had worn during my best mock test—I took a deep breath. I tied my hair up in a neat ponytail, my fingers slightly trembling as I adjusted my glasses. There was something almost sacred about result day, the way it carried a heavy stillness before the storm of emotions.

By the time I reached the living room, everyone had already gathered. Mom was pacing near the kitchen, pretending to be calm, but the way she kept wiping her hands on her dupatta gave her away. Dad was seated on the couch, sipping his tea, though his eyes flickered to me every few seconds. Rishi was there too, leaning against the wall, his arms crossed, looking entirely too relaxed for my liking.

"You've got this," he mouthed, giving me a small, confident nod.

Jai, Simie, and Apurva were sitting on the floor, their eyes glued to my laptop as I hesitantly placed it on the table. The CA Institute's website was already open, waiting for me to key in my registration number.

My hands were clammy as I typed it in, my breath catching in my throat as I hovered over the 'Submit' button. This was it.

Click.

The page took three agonizing seconds to load.

And then—it was there.

PASS

I stared at the word, my mind taking a second to process it. Then my eyes scanned further—cleared both groups. My marks exceeded my expectations. I had done it.

I had passed.

A sharp breath left my lips, and for a moment, I couldn't move. Then, the room erupted into chaos.

"She did it!" Simie screeched, throwing her arms around me.

"Of course, she did," Jai grinned, pulling me into a side hug.

Apurva was clapping excitedly while Mom and Dad were beaming with pride. Mom's eyes were misty as she cupped my face. "I knew you'd do it, beta. I'm so proud of you."

Before I could even react, Rishi grabbed me by the waist and lifted me off the ground, spinning me around as I yelped. "Rishi! Put me down!" I gasped between laughter.

"Nope! Not until it sinks in that you're a genius," he said, finally setting me back on my feet.

And then, as if the moment couldn't get any more surreal, he pulled out a box from behind the couch.

"You brought a cake?" I asked, half-laughing, half-shocked.

He smirked. "Of course. I knew you'd clear. I wasn't going to let you pass this milestone without a proper celebration."

It was a rich chocolate cake with 'Congratulations, CA Aarna in Making' written in elegant frosting. The sight of it, combined with the overwhelming emotions, made my eyes sting with unshed tears.

We cut the cake amidst cheers and laughter, the sweetness of the moment sinking deep into my bones. I wasn't just happy—I was glowing. I had made it past one of the hardest hurdles of my career.

Later that day, an email popped up on my phone.

Subject: Offer Letter - Deloitte Tax Department

My breath hitched. I opened it in a rush, scanning the words.

I had secured my articleship at Deloitte. In the Tax Department. Exactly where I had wanted to be.

I let out a shaky laugh, looking up at everyone who had now become my biggest cheerleaders.

Rishi raised an eyebrow. "Good news?"

I grinned. "Great news. I'm in Deloitte. Tax."

A fresh round of cheers followed, and at that moment, standing among the people who meant the most to me, I felt it.

I was in my perfect life era. And it was just the beginning.

63

RISHI

There are moments in life that feel almost cinematic—the kind where the music swells, the lighting is just right, and everything seems to fall into place. Clearing my CFA Level 1 was one of those moments. The hours of relentless studying, the sleepless nights spent buried in financial models, the anxiety of exam day—it had all led to this. And now, as I stood in my office, sipping on my coffee, I couldn't help but feel like I had finally stepped into the life I had always envisioned.

The best part? Aarna was right here with me.

We had both ended up working at the same firm—different departments, but the same building, same lunch breaks, same inside jokes about our coworkers. Some might call it fate, but I called it sheer perfection. Watching her stride into the office every morning in her crisp formals, her ID swinging around her neck, that determined glint in her eyes—it was a sight I could never get enough of.

Everything felt right. More than right. It felt like we had finally arrived at the future we used to dream about when we were younger, when stolen conversations on landlines and late-night exam prep were all we had. Now, we had careers, stability, and each other.

But just when you think life has settled into its perfect rhythm, something always comes along to throw you off balance.

It happened over dinner at home.

Mom and Dad had been exchanging knowing glances all evening, speaking in half sentences, waiting for the right moment. I should've known something was coming.

And then it did.

"So, Rishi..." My mom started, setting down her spoon. "Your dad and I have been talking."

I glanced up, raising a brow. "That's usually how marriages work."

My dad chuckled, but my mom didn't even crack a smile. "We think it's time you start considering settling down."

The words hit me like a gut punch.

I blinked. "Settling down?"

"Yes," my dad chimed in, ever the practical one. "You're doing well in your career, you've cleared CFA Level 1, and by next year, you'll be moving on to Level 2. It's a good time to think about the future."

The future. The one I had already planned—with Aarna.

I swallowed, my fingers tightening around the edge of the dining table. "And by 'consider settling down,' you mean?"

"We've started looking," my mom said simply. "For a girl."

My stomach turned. "A girl?"

"Yes, Rishi," she continued, oblivious to the storm raging inside me. "You know, someone from a good family, with similar values. We've spoken to a few people, and there are some great matches."

My head spun. Matches? Like some business deal being arranged without me even knowing?

I forced a breath. "I don't— I mean, I'm not—"

"We're not saying you have to get married tomorrow," my dad interrupted, sensing my discomfort. "Just meet a few people. Keep an open mind."

An open mind?

I already had someone.

And she was everything.

Aarna's laughter echoed in my mind, the way her eyes sparkled when she spoke about her dreams, the way she fit so effortlessly into my life. The idea of anyone else in her place felt wrong. Impossible.

But here I was, sitting across from my parents as they planned my future without even realizing that it had already been decided the moment Aarna walked back into my life.

I pushed my plate away, appetite gone. "I'll think about it."

It was a lie. Because there was nothing to think about.

There was only Aarna.

64

AARNA

Arranged marriage.

The words felt foreign in my head as I stared at my reflection in the mirror. My mother had insisted I wear something 'decent yet elegant,' so I had settled on a soft lavender kurti with intricate embroidery along the neckline. My lucky bracelet sat snugly on my wrist, a silent reminder that I had faced bigger things than this.

"Aarna, are you ready?" Mom called from outside my room.

I took a deep breath. "Coming."

I had no intention of actually saying yes to whoever my parents had picked out. I knew Rishi would be upset if he found out I was even entertaining this, which is exactly why I hadn't told him. He had his own battle to fight, and I wasn't going to add to his stress. I had already made up my mind—I was going to meet the guy, be polite, and then turn him down as graciously as possible.

We arrived at the restaurant, a cozy, well-lit place with an air of quiet sophistication. I spotted my parents, sitting across from another couple, engaged in polite conversation. And then, I turned my head toward the guy I was supposed to meet.

I almost choked.

Rishi.

Sitting there in a crisp navy blue shirt, his sleeves rolled up just enough to make my thoughts spiral, was the man I had spent years loving. His expression mirrored mine—stunned disbelief, eyes flickering with confusion before a slow realization set in.

Our parents wanted us to get married.

Of all the people in the world, of all the arranged meetings, fate had somehow dragged us into this particular mess.

I let out a small laugh, covering it with a cough as I sat down. My parents were too caught up in their conversation to notice my internal breakdown. Rishi, meanwhile, had schooled his expression into something almost amused.

"Why don't you two go talk for a while?" Rishi's mother suggested, smiling warmly.

"Yes, beta," my father added, "Get to know each other."

Oh, if only they knew.

Rishi stood up, giving me a small smirk as he gestured toward the outdoor seating area. I followed, biting my lip to keep from laughing at the absurdity of the situation. The moment we were out of earshot, I turned to him, arms crossed.

"So," I said, "care to explain why you're here?"

He scoffed. "I should be asking you that."

"I didn't tell you because I knew you'd get mad. But jokes on me, I guess. What are the odds?"

"Honestly? I came here planning to say no to whoever my parents picked," he admitted, running a hand through his hair. "But now..." he trailed off, tilting his head slightly, eyes twinkling with mischief. "I might reconsider."

I rolled my eyes, but I couldn't help the laugh that bubbled out. "Oh, shut up."

He grinned, taking a step closer. "You have to admit, this is hilarious. Our parents, thinking they're setting us up, when we—"

"—have been dancing around this for years?" I finished for him, shaking my head. "Yeah. It's unreal."

We stood there for a moment, staring at each other, the weight of our past, our present, and maybe—just maybe—our future settling around us. I had spent so much time thinking about the right timing, about how we would tell our families. But maybe, the universe had decided for us.

"So, what do we do now?" I asked.

Rishi smirked, sliding his hands into his pockets. "Well, we can go back inside and break their hearts... or, we can sit through this and see where it takes us."

I raised a brow. "Are you saying we go along with this?"

He shrugged. "What's the harm in letting them think they succeeded?"

I laughed, shaking my head. "You are unbelievable."

He leaned in slightly, voice dropping just enough to make my pulse stutter. "And yet, you're still here."

I rolled my eyes but smiled. Maybe, just maybe, the universe had finally gotten it right.

65

RISHI

The moment Aarna stepped into the hall, everything around me faded. It was as if time itself had taken a step back to admire her.

She wore a lilac lehenga that shimmered softly under the chandelier lights, embroidered with intricate silver patterns that seemed to dance as she moved. The skirt flared just enough to make her look effortlessly regal, and the delicate blouse had sheer, full sleeves, revealing glimpses of her warm skin beneath. The neckline was modest, yet elegant, accentuating the curve of her collarbones, where a dazzling diamond necklace rested—glowing, but not as much as she did. The dupatta was draped over one shoulder, pinned in place with an ornate brooch, and its sheer fabric flowed behind her like a whisper of a dream.

Her hair was styled in soft waves, cascading down her back, and a delicate maang tikka rested at the center of her forehead, complementing the sparkle in her kohl-rimmed eyes. Those eyes—brighter than the diamonds she wore—met mine, and for a brief moment, it felt like the entire world had been built just for this, just for us. Her lips, painted in a soft rose shade, curled into a knowing smile, and I swore my heart stumbled over itself.

I barely registered the people around us—the music, the chatter, the ceremony unfolding—because all I could focus on was her. Aarna. Mine.

When the time came to exchange rings, I slipped the diamond-studded band onto her finger, feeling her shiver slightly under my touch. She did the same for me, her fingers lingering against mine, as if we both wanted to stretch this moment forever. But then came the real test—the truth.

After the formalities, when our parents gathered around to celebrate, I knew we couldn't keep this from them any longer. Aarna and I exchanged a glance, and with an almost imperceptible nod, I cleared my throat.

"Mom, Dad, there's something we need to tell you."

The joy in their faces dimmed just slightly as my words settled in the air. Aarna's parents turned toward us, curious but calm. My own mother stiffened, her smile faltering. "What is it, Rishi?"

I reached for Aarna's hand, lacing my fingers with hers. "We've been together for a while now. This... this isn't just an arranged marriage for us. We chose each other a long time ago."

There was silence. A tense, thick silence that stretched too long for comfort. My father's brows furrowed, my mother's lips pressed into a thin line.

"This isn't right," my mother finally spoke. "If you were already involved, why didn't you tell us?"

"We wanted to," Aarna said softly. "But we didn't know how to. And honestly, we never thought things would work out this way."

My mother shook her head. "Rishi, marriage is not just about love. It's about families, traditions, responsibilities—"

Aarna's mom placed a gentle hand on my mother's arm, smiling knowingly. "And isn't it even better that this is both love and arranged? They have history, yes. But they also have a future, one they've built themselves."

My mother looked at Aarna's mom, then at me, and then at Aarna. She took a deep breath. My father exhaled and finally smiled. "Well," he said, his voice lighter. "If fate wanted you two together this badly, who are we to argue?"

Relief flooded through me, and I felt Aarna squeeze my hand. The tension in the room dissolved, replaced by cheers and claps.

Music started playing again, and the evening melted into a blur of laughter, dance, and endless photographs. Our friends twirled us into the celebrations, teasing, cheering, pulling us apart only to push us back together. The night was filled with love, new relationships forming between families, and an undeniable sense of destiny unfolding before us.

As Aarna leaned into me while our parents hugged each other, she whispered, "This really is our perfect story, isn't it?"

I looked at her, my future, my forever, and smirked. "Oh, Aarna. This is just the beginning."

66

AARNA

The moment I saw the word Pass flashing on my CA Final results screen, my heart nearly stopped. It felt surreal—like I had climbed a mountain so high that I was now touching the sky. My hands were shaking, my throat was dry, and for a second, I forgot how to breathe.

And then, the screams erupted.

Simie grabbed me, jumping in excitement, while Jai fist-bumped the air. Apurva hugged me so tight that I almost lost my balance. My parents had tears in their eyes—tears of pride, of relief, of years of prayers being answered. My father, usually a man of few words, simply nodded with a proud smile and patted my head, a gesture that meant the world to me. My mother hugged me, whispering, "You did it, beta. I always knew you would."

Rishi was already holding a cake in his hands—because of course, he knew I was going to pass. He walked over with that easy confidence, his eyes filled with pride. "I had a feeling I'd need this," he smirked, handing me the knife.

Rolling my eyes but grinning like an idiot, I cut the cake while everyone cheered. Rishi smeared a little frosting on my nose, and before I could react, he pulled me into a hug.

It wasn't just a congratulatory hug; it was a promise—of forever, of standing beside me through everything, of a love that was as certain as my dreams.

**

Life was a whirlwind after that. I barely had time to soak in my success before wedding preparations took over. The house was flooded with relatives, my phone never stopped buzzing, and every other day, my mom dragged me to a boutique, a jeweler, or a decorator.

"Beta, we need to finalize your mehendi design today," she said one evening, scrolling through Pinterest. "And also the floral arrangements."

"I have a meeting in an hour, Mom," I reminded her.

"You're getting married in a month, Aarna. Priorities."

I laughed, shaking my head. The house was brimming with chaos, but it was the kind of chaos I had always dreamt of.

And then came the sangeet.

The venue was decked in fairy lights and fresh flowers, music pulsated in the air, and my entire world—family, friends, colleagues—was there to celebrate Rishi and me. I wore an intricately embroidered silver and lilac lehenga, my diamond jewelry sparkling under the lights. My mehendi-stained hands trembled slightly as I adjusted my bangles, but my excitement overpowered the nerves.

Rishi looked like a dream in his deep blue sherwani, his eyes never leaving me the entire night. Every time I caught him staring, he'd smirk, making my stomach flip. The way he held my hand, the way he twirled me on the dance floor—it felt like we were in our own world, a world where only we existed.

And then, my gaze fell on him.

Ayaan.

For a moment, everything slowed down. He stood at the far end of the hall, talking to someone I didn't recognize. He hadn't changed much—still the same self-assured stance, the same charming demeanor. But there was no power in his presence anymore. No fear. No anxiety. Nothing.

I turned to Simie, who followed my gaze and stiffened. "What the hell is he doing here?"

"Probably a guest from Rishi's side," I guessed. My heart was calm, my mind at ease. There was no anger, no fear, no hesitation. Ayaan was just another face in the crowd.

I found Rishi's gaze in an instant. He had noticed too. His jaw tightened, his fingers flexing, but the moment our eyes met, his expression softened. He knew. He always knew.

Minutes later, Rishi pulled me aside, his voice low. "Are you okay?"

I smiled, running my hand over his arm. "More than okay."

His lips pressed into a thin line before he nodded. "Good."

And with that, we walked back into our celebration, hand in hand, ready to step into the future. Together.

67

RISHI

The sangeet night was nothing short of magical, and Aarna—God, Aarna—she was breathtaking.

She wore a royal blue lehenga that shimmered under the golden fairy lights, the intricate silver embroidery glistening with every graceful movement she made. The blouse had a delicate off-shoulder cut, revealing just a hint of collarbone, and the sheer dupatta cascaded over her arms like a whisper. Her diamond jewelry sparkled like tiny stars against her smooth skin, and her hair, styled in soft waves, framed her face perfectly. The moment I saw her, I forgot every single person in the room.

Tonight was about us.

The sangeet began with laughter, teasing, and a whirlwind of performances. The stage was set, and our friends had planned an entire sequence of dances. Jai and Simie started the night with an energetic performance on Koi Mil Gaya, getting everyone hyped up. Apurva and Raj followed, setting the stage on fire with their synchronized moves.

Then came our moment.

Aarna and I stepped onto the stage, the spotlight washing over us as Perfect by Ed Sheeran played. She looked at me with those mesmerizing eyes, and I pulled her closer, leading her into a slow waltz. The world melted away as we moved together, each step effortless, as if we had been dancing forever.

And then, the beat changed. The transition into Tum Se Hi sent a wave of nostalgia rushing through me. It was our song—the one that had been playing in the background of our tangled love story for years. The way Aarna smiled at me in that moment, with pure, unguarded happiness, made my chest tighten. I twirled her around, the hem of her lehenga fanning out like a dream, and when she returned to me, I held her close, our foreheads touching for just a second before the final note played.

The cheers and applause were deafening, but all I could hear was the pounding of my heart.

As the night carried on, I found myself standing near the bar when I heard a familiar voice behind me.

"Congratulations, Rishi."

I turned, my expression hardening instantly. Ayaan.

He extended his hand, a polite smile on his face. There was no malice, no arrogance—just a simple congratulation. For a second, I considered ignoring him. But then I glanced at Aarna across the room, laughing with Simie, completely unaffected by his presence.

So, I shook his hand. "Thanks."

Whatever had happened in the past didn't matter anymore. Aarna was mine, and nothing—not even ghosts from the past—could change that.

The night continued with more dance, music, and joy, and as I pulled Aarna into one last dance under the soft glow of the chandeliers, I realized something.

This wasn't just a celebration of our wedding.

This was a celebration of us. Of the years we had fought, loved, lost, and found our way back to each other.

And in this moment, with Aarna in my arms, life had never felt more perfect.

68

AARNA

The day I had dreamt of since I was a little girl had finally arrived.

I stood in front of the mirror, my heart pounding as I took in my reflection. The dream pink lehenga I had chosen shimmered under the soft glow of the vanity lights, the intricate silver embroidery weaving stories of love and eternity. The sheer dupatta, adorned with tiny pearls, rested lightly on my head, cascading down my back like a veil of moonlight. My jewelry—a choker encrusted with diamonds and pastel pink gemstones, matching dangling earrings, and a delicate maang tikka that rested right at the center of my forehead—added to the ethereal look. Bangles of gold and blush pink clinked softly against each other as I adjusted them, my mehendi-stained hands trembling slightly with anticipation. My kaleere hung delicately from my wrists, swaying with every little movement.

My hair was styled in a voluminous bun, decorated with baby's breath flowers and tiny pearl pins, a touch of elegance to complement the grandeur of the day. My makeup was kept soft yet striking—blushed cheeks, kohl-rimmed eyes that held the dreams of a lifetime, and lips painted the perfect shade of rose. I felt like a princess, no, a queen, walking towards her destiny.

And that destiny was waiting for me at the mandap.

As I stepped out of the bridal suite, my heart swelled with emotion. My parents stood beside me, my mother's eyes brimming with unshed tears while my father gave me a reassuring nod. The wedding venue was breathtaking, adorned with cascading flowers in hues of blush pink, ivory, and gold, fairy lights twinkling like stars, and candles flickering softly in the evening breeze. It felt like stepping into a dream, one where love was the only reality.

Then, the music started.

'Teri Ore... Teri Ore...'

The moment the first note of the song played, a rush of emotions surged through me. Holding onto my father's arm, I walked down the aisle, my eyes locked onto Rishi's. He stood under the beautifully decorated mandap, dressed in an ivory sherwani with intricate gold embroidery, a matching safa tied perfectly on his head, with a bejeweled brooch at the center. His eyes held a thousand emotions, but the most evident of them all was love. Love so deep and consuming that it made my chest tighten.

He looked nothing short of regal, his sharp features softened by the flickering firelight. The string of pearls around his neck complemented the elegance he carried so effortlessly. He was the man of my dreams, the one I had always imagined standing there, waiting for me, and now, it was real.

I let out a shaky breath as I reached him, feeling my heart hammer against my ribs. He extended his hand towards me, and without hesitation, I placed mine in his. His grip was firm yet gentle, his thumb grazing over my fingers, a silent reassurance that we were in this together.

The varmala ceremony began, and laughter erupted from our friends and family as Rishi teasingly pulled back, making me reach higher to put the garland around his neck. I rolled my eyes, but the laughter in my heart bubbled over as I finally managed to slip it over him. When it was his turn, he wasted no time, placing the varmala around my neck and then whispering, "Now you're mine, officially."

Fireworks exploded in the sky, a burst of golden and pink illuminating the night as cheers and applause echoed around us. It was a moment of pure magic, of colors dancing in the sky as if celebrating our union. I closed my eyes for a second, soaking it all in, memorizing the feeling of this once-in-a-lifetime moment.

The rituals commenced, each one tying us together in a bond that transcended time. As we sat side by side, performing the sacred rituals, I felt the weight of the moment settle in. This was not just about love; this was about promises, about lifetimes entwining. When Rishi filled the parting of my hair with sindoor, I shivered at the realization that I was now his in every sense of the word. And when he tied the mangalsutra around my neck, my heart swelled with a kind of happiness I had never known before.

As the final pheras were completed, and the priest announced us as husband and wife, I turned to look at Rishi, my husband. My lips trembled as I smiled, and he reached forward, tucking a stray strand of hair behind my ear. "Mrs. Aarna Rishi Mehra," he murmured, his voice filled with a mixture of pride, love, and pure adoration.

I laughed softly. "That sounds... surreal."

"You're mine now," he whispered, his fingers lacing through mine, tightening as if to never let go.

"And you're mine," I whispered back, my voice steady, certain.

As the celebrations continued, we were surrounded by the people who had been a part of our journey—the ones who had seen us grow, fall, fight, and find our way back to each other. The music played, the night sparkled, and love, in all its grandeur, wrapped around us like a warm embrace.

I danced my way into Rishi's arms that night, the echoes of our laughter mixing with the soft rustling of the wind. I was his, and he was mine.

Forever.

69

RISHI

Bringing Aarna home as my wife felt surreal. It wasn't just about the wedding, the rituals, or the promises made under a canopy of lights—it was about the quiet moments that followed, the ones where reality settled in. The ones where I realized that she was mine, in every sense of the word, and that this was just the beginning of our forever.

The first morning in our home, Aarna was already up before me. I found her in the kitchen, dressed in a simple peach kurta, her mangalsutra resting against her collarbone, the light sindoor in her parting a soft reminder of the vows we had taken. She was making tea, humming under her breath, completely at ease. My mother sat at the dining table, watching her with pure affection.

"You didn't have to wake up this early," I said, walking up behind her, my arms circling her waist instinctively.

She turned her head slightly, smiling. "Someone had to make breakfast, Mr. Rishi. I'm officially a part of this household now."

I pressed a kiss to the top of her head before pulling away. "And what do you think I've been doing for the past few years? Surviving on air?"

My mom chuckled. "She's just excited, beta. Let her be."

Excited was an understatement. Aarna had always been driven, a perfectionist, and now that she was officially here, she wanted to make sure she played her role perfectly. But in our home, there was no need for expectations—only love.

Mornings became our quiet tradition. Aarna would prepare breakfast, her hair still damp from the shower, the aroma of freshly made parathas or poha filling the kitchen. My mom packed tiffins for both of us—lunch neatly divided into two steel containers, each wrapped with a napkin as if we were kids going to school again. And every evening, when I came home earlier than Aarna, I would take over the kitchen, making dinner before she walked in, exhausted but smiling.

It was a routine that made my heart full.

One evening, as she walked into the house, her shoulders slumped from a long day at work, I was already plating dinner—her favorite, paneer butter masala with naan.

She sniffed the air dramatically and sighed. "God, I married the right man."

I smirked. "That was never in question."

She slipped her arms around my waist from behind, resting her cheek against my back. "Thank you for this. For always making life easy for me."

I turned, cupping her face. "You work just as hard. We balance each other, Aaru. That's what this is about."

She smiled up at me, her eyes filled with something I could only describe as home.

Even my mom, who had always been the most important woman in my life, had now found a new favorite—Aarna. If I wasn't home, the two of them would sit together, talking for hours, sharing recipes, shopping plans, and even teasing me whenever I joined them. It was effortless, the way Aarna blended into my world, as if she had always belonged there.

One Saturday morning, I woke up to the sound of laughter from the kitchen. I walked in, rubbing my eyes, to find Aarna and my mom making laddoos together, the kitchen a mess of flour, sugar, and misplaced spoons.

"You're both conspiring against me," I said, grabbing a piece of dough.

My mom swatted my hand. "Go freshen up, Rishi. You're not getting any of these until they're ready."

Aarna smirked. "Or until you do the dishes."

I groaned. "Marriage is a scam."

Aarna threw a handful of flour at me, and just like that, the kitchen turned into a war zone.

Life with her was full of moments like these. Little things. Breakfasts together. Late-night conversations. Shared looks across the dinner table. A warm hand slipping into mine when no one was watching.

I had always loved her, but now, I was living in that love. And it was perfect.

70

AARNA

Five years.

It's been five whole years since I walked down that aisle in my dream pink lehenga, with "Teri Ore" playing in the background, my heart racing as I reached Rishi. Five years since I became his wife, since we vowed to stand by each other through everything life had to offer.

And today, as I stand on the balcony of our home, sipping my evening coffee, I feel nothing but contentment. The warm glow of Diwali lights flickers against the soft evening sky, and laughter echoes from inside our house. It's been years, yet every Diwali feels more magical than the last.

A gentle breeze brushes past me, carrying the scent of fresh marigolds and the subtle aroma of Rishi's cologne. I close my eyes for a moment, letting it all sink in. My life is everything I ever dreamed of—and more.

Inside, our home is brimming with people and love. Both our families have gathered to celebrate Diwali together, just like every year. The living room is bathed in warm golden hues from the diyas, the air rich with the fragrance of sweets, incense, and laughter. My mother-in-law is busy arranging the puja thali, while my mom is making sure the kids don't set off too many crackers at once.

Kids.

Aarish and Aarika—our little stars, our whole world.

Aarish, our four-year-old boy, is the exact replica of Rishi. The same eyes, the same mischievous grin that could melt anyone's heart. He's dressed in a tiny blue kurta and white pajama, running around excitedly, asking his grandfather to light another firework for him. Aarika, our two-year-old princess, is my shadow. She clings to my saree, her chubby hands wrapped around my fingers as she watches her big brother in fascination. Dressed in a tiny pink lehenga, with soft curls bouncing as she moves, she is the perfect blend of me and Rishi.

Rishi steps onto the balcony, a soft smile playing on his lips. "Caught you daydreaming again, Mrs. Aarna?" he teases, wrapping an arm around my waist.

I lean into him, sighing happily. "Just taking it all in. Look at them, Rishi. Look at our family. We made it."

His grip tightens slightly, and I hear the warmth in his voice. "Yeah, we did."

For a moment, we just stand there, watching our family inside, the flickering lights reflecting in our eyes. My father and his father are deep in conversation, probably discussing stocks or real estate. My mother and his mother are exchanging sweet recipes, their bond having grown even stronger over the years. Simie and Jai are playing cards with our cousins, laughter erupting every few minutes. It's a home filled with love, just the way we always wanted.

Rishi's fingers intertwine with mine. "Remember our first Diwali together?" he asks.

I chuckle, nodding. "Of course. You burnt your kurta while lighting a rocket, and I spent the entire night scolding you for being so careless."

He laughs, shaking his head. "And now look at us. Responsible parents, homeowners, professionals. Who would've thought?"

I nudge him playfully. "I did."

He turns to look at me, his expression softening. "I couldn't have done any of it without you, Aarna."

I tilt my head, pretending to think. "Well, I did make you the luckiest man alive."

Rishi rolls his eyes but pulls me closer, dropping a gentle kiss on my forehead. "That, you did."

Inside, Aarish suddenly calls out, "Mumma, Papa, come fast! We have to do the aarti!"

I smile, squeezing Rishi's hand one last time before we step back inside. The entire family gathers around the small temple in our living room, the diya's flame flickering steadily as we sing the aarti together. Aarika claps her tiny hands to the rhythm, while Aarish holds onto Rishi's kurta, singing along in his sweet, innocent voice.

As we finish the prayer, I look around at the people I love the most, at the home we've built together, at the life we've created. It's not perfect, but it's ours. And that's more than enough.

I glance at Rishi, finding him already looking at me, his eyes reflecting the same emotions swirling in my heart. Love, gratitude, and an unbreakable bond that has only strengthened over the years.

We made it.

And we always will.

ﭗﭗﭗ

A Note to My Readers

Tangled Hearts is more than just a story; it's a testament to the kind of love that withstands time, obstacles, and uncertainties. It's about growing together, navigating life's unexpected twists, and finding home in another person.

At its core, this book reflects the beauty of fate, the strength of choices, and the warmth of relationships built on trust and understanding.

If there's one thing I hope *Tangled Hearts* leaves you with, it's this: True love isn't just about finding someone. It's about choosing them, over and over again.

Thank you for being a part of this journey.

WITH LOVE, AASKA